women behaving badly

Feisty Flash Fiction Stories

International Edition

For John —
Enjoy the stories and
keep writing!
Cynthia Price Reedy

women behaving badly

Feisty Flash Fiction Stories

International Edition

Edited by Wanda Wade Mukherjee and Sharlene Baker

TPJ

The Paper Journey Press
Sojourner Publishing, Inc.• North Carolina

WOMEN BEHAVING BADLY:
FEISTY FLASH FICTION STORIES

The Paper Journey Press: http://thepaperjourney.com
First trade paperback edition.
Manufactured in the United States of America.
International Standard Book Number (ISBN) 0-9701726-3-X

"April Fool" first appeared in *The Drexel Online Journal*, copyright 2000.
Reprinted by permission of the author.

For Debbie Ann: once lost but now found.
                    W.W.M.

For my real mother, who saw fit to circle me with her arms
and hug *hard.*
                    S.B.

Acknowledgments

My thanks to Frank for pitching in a pinch.

Many accolades to my husband and soul mate Subir, who has tirelessly supported me on one adventure after another.

And

A nod of appreciation to G. A: Your generous gifts of spirit and integrity make you Citizen of the Millennium in my book.

W.W.M

My deepest gratitude to Nancy Keppler, for sharing with me her endless supply of support and encouragement, and for inspiring the title of this book with her lifetime of rabble-rousing for all the right reasons.

S.B.

 **Introduction**

Most writers seek to find meaning in the human condition—to capture the universal heart dwelling at the core of us all. Yet those who write the short story go a step further; tell the story of a life with the precision and brevity of a poem.

Short story writers are perhaps some of the most misunderstood and underrated of those who put pen to paper. Despite the lack of a viable mainstream market, many continue their quest for that *one* character, *one* plot which will explain the *all* to ourselves.

We wanted to showcase the talents of short story writers from around the world who excel in the genre of flash fiction. So when we sent out a call for short-short stories with the theme "Women Behaving Badly" we puzzled over what might blow across our desks.

I was hoping for heroines in every sense of the word, but I didn't want heroics. It didn't matter if the author was male or female: I was on the lookout for stories whose protagonist was someone who had a little bit of you and me at her center.

Stories of all plots and styles arrived. They came from Last Wagon Drive, Tollgate Gardens, and towns in Canada with names impossible to pronounce. We had envelopes from North Dakota and emails from South Africa. And from the moment we opened the first envelope we knew we had hit the jackpot.

The fictional women of these feisty stories behaved in ways that could only be described as, well, "bad" by society's standards. Our naughty girls surprised us in more ways than we had ever envisioned.

A particular haunting story is Robin Skyler's "Shoestring"; the story of a young woman overwhelmed with life, teetering on the edge of losing hold. She is in stark contrast to Car(o)l C. Smith's protagonist in "She Swam the Channel," a champion swimmer desperately fighting to hold onto her life despite a single, costly mistake. The death of a child and its psychic aftermath in "April Fool" by Robert Wallace is *the story* at its classic best. And Liesl Jobson's "Recipe for Sedition" brings home the reality of AIDS in South Africa and the shattering desire of a young girl who was married off too young to a man too old.

There are other characters more real than life itself. Julie Ann Jones' Germaine in "Working Girl" wants desperately to get her daughter out of foster care, but finds it impossible to overcome her innate self-destructiveness. And, then there's that impish pubescent tomboy created by author Calabrese, who can't make heads or tales of the "hammock" she's supposed to wear between her legs in "Gees, I Never Woulda Guessed.

I certainly can't leave out Sean Aden Lovelace's Peggy Guggenheim, in her scandalous quest for chocolate éclairs as the world explodes around her during the fall of Paris. Somehow it seems fitting that Peggy should anchor a collection of short stories fore and aft.

I'm pleased to say that our writers rose to the challenge: they found heroines among those who were less than heroic. These stories may be about "women behaving badly," yet they exemplify the humanness within us all.

.

Wanda Wade Mukherjee
Wake Forest, 2004

 **Table of Contents**

Women Behaving Badly

Feisty Flash Fiction Stories

Peggy Guggenheim Visits Her Favorite Question

Sean Aden Lovelace

Q: "How many husbands have you had, Mrs. Guggenheim?"
A: "D'you mean my own, or other people's?"

There is one privately owned palazzo along the Grand Canal, and only one privately owned gondola left in the entire city. Mine. It spent the morning picking up an American graduate student from the train station at Santa Lucia.

She's not here for the city, so dazzling it seems to belong to a better, truer, deeper blue and green planet, but rather to interview me, for her dissertation, something about gender studies and modern art, which I find flattering, and then again frightening: I am a relic, something to see, like my paintings.

She refuses a drink, noting the early hour, but maybe later a vodka martini. I tell her there is no such thing as a vodka martini. She compliments my dogs, but not individually, only as a group, something about their energy. She's pretty; all the young American women are pretty now, and I feel a melting ice of jealousy in my stomach. I should be over that but I'm not. As I discuss the canals and viaducts of Venice, she nods and smiles, but not with her eyes. Her eyes don't smile ... and so? She is perfectly nice, is what I'm saying.

I mix my drink, my movements practiced over the slender glasses (high art, in my opinion), the crushed ice, and tell her about how my first husband thought preparing a martini was some great life metaphor, the proper portions, the presentation—it's one of the reasons our marriage didn't last. While he drank for philosophical reasons, I drank to get tight.

"Wait, wait, wait, say that again," she says, fumbling with her purse, a Gucci the color of wet sand. She holds a tape recorder, sleek and black like a packet of French cigarettes.

I don't say it again.

She sets up her recorder and asks of Picasso and I answer: technical, difficult, invisible inside. She continues, and I see the only way of nudging her from subjects I find nauseating is to create discomfort. And so I say loudly, "He found me stupid and rich and stupid."

She asks of Pollock and I tell two of the five usual anecdotes and then, "He would urinate most anywhere, including my fireplace."

She mentions my sisters, their renowned beauty, and I reply, "It only made me feel more repulsive." Emboldened for a few intriguing seconds, she digs deeper, and I follow up with: "One died while giving birth, the other dropped her two infant sons sixteen stories from a New York rooftop."

There are no further questions and she has a bowl of Brusciuvia, three buttery slices of Semolina bread, and finally a drink, a martini—as in gin, darling. I mix two, smiling as she bird-sips and shoulder-shudders her way along. She glances about the room, at my paintings, and I give her a few general details, names, dates, a Plexiglas placard at a museum.

Then she asks about sex.

"I like the word fuck. I do, and I like to fuck. I can't say why. Something about incursions, expulsions, the mixing of faces, sexes, all the grappling ... there's something in the falling, the utter dark falling of the orgasm. I dedicated so much of my life to it ... I really can't say why. Maybe it's everything modern, all of it, its toll—alienation, analysis. Exhausting self-analysis ...

"What I mean by alienation is how I've felt alone. You understand? I have money so I can always have people, but they can't be me, think like me, these nights when I can't sleep, when I have Pietro, my gondolier, take me outside, out there, floating the canals, listening to the moon crackle ... or sitting here and thinking about my death-day. The way it marches down the calendar, marching, like the Nazis ... We all have a death-day, you know, dear, like a birthday, but, well, rather different ... I mean with sex I feel—or I felt—immersed, in the Other, fucking the Other, and all those whirring darts of pleasure/pain/whatever you want to label it, were maybe me, collecting myself, gathering up—not being alone, for once, a few seconds ... the orgasm ... or maybe I'm crazy.

"Or drunk. You've done your reading and you think here she is, drunk. Talking rot. But I'm not drunk, and I don't think you know anxiety. I'm not talking about late night studying for some little exam. No. I'm talking about marriage as a tedious, suffocating cage; about outliving your daughters; about every artist that takes your money, all of them waiting to get a name so they can never mention yours again. Yes ... I'm talking about suicide and murder. About Nazis. Nazis, for God's sake, and why? ... Don't be fooled—Yes, I'm a Venetian, now, but always an American. I fled Paris. Fled acquaintances, people in trouble. Serious trouble, if you understand me. I flee my anxieties, you see? With drink, sex ... you know, with money.

"But, no, I'm not drunk. And I'm not feeling sexy anymore. I suppose similarities exist: you do it for years, decades swim by, and you reflect on it all, for some pattern, some daily motivation for pouring a drink, for finding someone, someone to fuck, someone different than who you are fucking. Who knows why? A gear or cog inside just slips its, its what?—its bearing? I don't know the word. Maybe I don't know what I'm saying. Maybe. Well, there's analysis for you—the world's largest I don't know.

"I mean what are we doing here, dear?"

No reply, from either of us. She stares at the recorder, tilts it in her fingers, frowns, presses a button, mumbles something about the tape. I beckon her to the window, a wide glass wall, the sun a smeary ball of orange, melting, splintering into canals, glinting off the byways and eddies and cross-running tides of the lagoon, light thrown awry, refracted, diamonds tossed across a fractured jigsaw of bluish green.

"What do you think?" I say.

She shrugs. "It's like a picture."

I see our reflections in the window, a gull wheeling nearby, the sun, and feel a softening inside. Strange: I feel an urge to see myself in her. But why? I glance down to the quay, to the gondola being readied—soon my visitor must return to her hotel, and then to Milan, to interview a young lady who makes art from discarded automobile engines.

"And what do you think of Pietro?" I ask her.

"Who?" She turns from the window and yawns, immediately

apologizing, pleading the heavy bread and the late martini, and then, while collecting her things, tells me of her recent readings of Venice, about how the city is doomed, always was doomed to sink into the sea, and this the citizens' fault, their negligence, building on shifting sandbars and precarious wetlands as if it were terra firma—creating their very lives on sand, like so many—

"Goodnight," I tell her, and her eyes flicker, her face losing a bit of glow, its symmetry, and from her lips an uncertain mumbling as she heads to the doorway. In silence I watch from the window as Pietro takes her hand and guides her into the gondola, he smiling, she clearly not smiling, not smiling at Pietro, and she turns for a last glance and I am across the room, mixing a martini, stirring it slowly, slowly, so as not to bruise the gin.

What She Took Out of Here

Ariana-Sophia Kartsonis

Here being a town that took everything out of her. Out being the next place.

What she took was seven wishes and seven carousel ponies to ride them out. She took a bus, an umbrella, a stick of black licorice and what was left of her heart. She took nothing more from anyone. Then she took off.

Romeo was a dark-skinned boy that danced up from the heat-shimmer in the highway just ahead. She took that vision, too. That Romeo, that heat-shadow mirage, that trick of the eyes that was him and nothing else beautiful from that place back there that she left behind. She folded her self like an origami bird and she strung it up where the wind was likely to set it soaring. She took a twig and some twine and the paperbird and her heart full of darkskinned boys and made a mobile of them to hang in the window of a life up ahead.

She was hopeful. Half-hearted but hopeful.

Back there were bad dreams and vacancies with nothing to fill them. Back there her joy hung like a cheap suit on the frame of her. Up ahead was hot-shiny with chance. Up there was every-where she'd never been and everything she'd never loved. But was knee-deep in. About-To and shoulder deep in Yes.

Seven carousel ponies were seen running down Highway 48. A flash of gold painted eyes and plastic flowered bridles gave them away. That and the peach-colored mare with her candy-eyed foal rolling by as if it were nothing to gallop with a brass pole jammed through your belly.

But back to our girl.

Let's say that the world changed clothes for her. That she could pinpoint herself on a map of the world and say, "This is where I meant to be. I'm here—really here—no there about it."

That if Romeo rose up from the never-there puddles of make-believe rivers up ahead, she would know him as the boy she left home for, the boy she'd call her own. Pretend for a while that our girl could choose a town, a boy, a somewhere, some life and move in, build a house. Learn that word called Stay. Ask nothing more of the sphere-songs than a little amplification, a little syncopation. A heart that plays half-time, plays hard and plays well.

Bookish

Brandy Foster

I met Felix in the Madison Street Library, in the stacks. I was holding *Emma*, debating whether it was too soon for a reread, when I looked up and saw a slim young gentleman with a copy of Flaubert's *Sentimental Education*. Though I was married, and though I knew better, I couldn't help but notice that he was my favorite type; thick, shaggy brown hair swept across a tender brow, intent chocolate eyes burning into mine behind wire rims, his Adam's apple bobbing up and down his slim white neck. He was a cross between Gilbert Blythe and Marius Pontmercy.

Ever bold, I affected an exquisite pose as I reached toward the B's. Withdrawing a shabbily-bound volume, I gracefully thrust it toward him.

"Excuse me, but I couldn't help but noticing your interest in Flaubert. May I recommend *Cousin Bette*?" I inquired, allowing a faint blush to paint my cheeks.

"Ah, Bal—zac," He knew my game immediately, of course.

And so, it began. We took the only sensible course, what with me being married; we went to Starbucks. Over double espressos, we exalted over Flaubert, though I preferred *Madame Bovary*. I dazzled him with my discourse on Flaubert's treatment of the bourgeoisie. He coyly mentioned Balzac's obsession with human vice. This time my blush was as red as Anne Shirley's hair.

That night, I mentioned to my husband that I had joined a new book club.

Felix and I enjoyed our first spat the very next week. We were revealing our most intimate thoughts, when he suddenly looked incredulous that I felt such admiration for Thomas Hardy.

"He's so insistently depressing. I mean, he's dark without any redeeming quality of style or plot. He weighs on my soul," Felix pulled back from me a little, taking a bitter sip of his espresso. I had to act fast; he was attacking my critical astuteness.

"Felix, think about what you're saying! How can you criticize Hardy? I mean, Tess, Felix, think about Tess." He still looked dubious, unshakable. There was only one thing to do. "You know, I've always felt a little like Jude, myself. You know, bad marriage, thwarted hopes, all that? 'The hell of conscious failure' bit?" I leaned back as I said it, hoping that my brows were forming that cool detachment that Kate Croy pulls off.

His look was priceless.

I blush to say it, but from then on, we were a little bit risqué, often downright rompy. We were all over Dumasì; sometimes we would bask in Wilde and the other decadents. Those were golden times. Sometimes, he was my Mr. Darcy, and I fancied that he was going to whisk me to Pemberly. Other times, he was much more like D'Artagnan in Milady's chamber.

We began exchanging little tokens of our ... esteem. He surprised me with *Gatsby*, and the next time we met, I left him with my cherished *Les Liaisons Dangereuses*.

Our little "book club" met for about six months, always within the chaste confines of the 4th Street Starbucks. That last time, I was early, chewing on my horned rims, trying to smooth my long, rayon skirt. I had accidentally ironed a stubborn crease into it in my haste to meet Felix.

As soon as I saw him, I knew something was up. He came away from the counter with his hands wrapped around a single, fat-free latte. I tried not to let my apprehension show as I averted my gaze from his cup to his eyes. He seemed nervous.

"So, how're your kids?" he asked, for the first time in our acquaintance.

"Uh, they're OK."

"OK?"

"Yeah." I was without words.

"Um, I have to tell you that I am, um ... going away," he said at last.

"Really? How nice." For the first time in my life, I'd wished that I could contrive Lydia Bennet's superficial gaiety.

"Uh, yeah. I've taken a job in Wallace. I start next week." I just nodded my head, knowing my face was turning splotchy with unshed tears. "It's a day job, so I won't be able to meet you any more."

"Well," I tried to say as I attempted to exhale and place a false smile on my face.

"I've enjoyed discussing literature with you," he said as he rose to walk out of my life. He reached inside his jacket and placed a book on the table between us, his eyes steady on mine. Then, he left.

I waited until he cleared the door, then I reached for the book. I gave a little smile, for it was Graham Greene's *End of the Affair*.

Sometimes, I think about Felix. What we shared was great—I mean, he really *got* me. And, it was nice to be had.

Shoestring

Robin Skyler

She's tried before to explain it. She doesn't know how to explain it to herself. But she knows it's the same thing again, just something about her, the same thing that always keeps her from holding on.

It makes her think of the first time she quit smoking, cold turkey, once and for all. She quit for four months and that's long enough; long enough to know you don't need it any more. Everybody seemed so surprised when she started again, and she couldn't manage to explain: she had smoked a cigarette. She smoked one cigarette (which she did not have to do) and she lost her hold, and she couldn't get it back.

It's like when you're walking in the rain, she thinks. She was out walking in the rain for some time this evening, the same freezing rain she can still hear on the roof outside her window. It may have been two hours she walked. It was long enough for her jaw to ache from the cold, long enough for the water to soak through her clothes and her skin. She still drips on the tiled floor, in a puddle surrounding her pale and nerveless feet.

When you walk in the rain you're fine, she thinks, until your shoes come unlaced for the first time. A loose shoestring on wet pavement, dragging, soggy—that cannot be recovered. You can tie it, but it won't hold. Once it loses its grip that first time, once it's wet, you're bound to go on tying it again every other minute. And that's that, for the rest of the day; a wet shoestring is no good to anybody until it's had a day under the radiator, and it's ready to start over.

Her hands grip the sides of the old sink and she stares at the mirror, at her own dark wet hair hanging cold and disordered around her face. Her eyes do not look like her eyes.

She has so much to answer for, she tells herself, a life that reduces to a long string of downfalls. If she could just tell them this one thing …

Beginning is easy, always was easy. She's forever starting things. As a child she started clubs, started piano lessons; later she started friendships. She started biking every Saturday, and loved it; it felt good. If anyone asks her she says she means to get back to it. Later she started cooking for her roommates every few days. She bought a telescope. She started reading the Old Testament. Everything goes splendidly well at first; she's as reliable as anyone could ask until something makes her slip the first time.

It's hard not to see the same pattern in her finances, her studies; she asks herself how she can suppose it won't define her career, and has no answer. If she cannot master a trade, she has no way out of her tenuous lifestyle; if she cannot keep up with her classes she may never find a trade. And if all these simple things are too much for her, how dare she even imagine motherhood?

She knows no reason why things should be this way. Anybody else can survive a setback, get back on track, and keep going. Nobody even understands the shape of the problem. She can't remember any particular beginning; it's as though she just got off on the wrong foot somewhere early in her life. It is an intrinsic part of her identity; she is the woman who fails when she most desperately needs not to.

Philadelphia was to be her new beginning, a new job and a new degree, a time to start everything over again all at once. It worked; it worked wonderfully, and she was happily busy with her work, and she kept abreast of everything without trouble.

Until tomorrow.

Tomorrow she has a midterm, and she cannot pass it; already it's too late to pass. She's done nothing to prepare. She knew the exam was coming. She could be studying now, should be, should get up in time to walk in at nine-thirty and salvage what she can. Should stay up all night, maybe. It might make a difference. She should be trying, even if it can't make a difference. Even if it's too late.

Her unfamiliar eyes stare back across the sink at her from the mirrored door of the medicine cabinet, dark resentful eyes set in pale skin, tangled hair, cold, still dripping. She knows too well how it will go after the first fall. If she lets this midterm go, it means the course; she will not be able to save it. If she lets a course go in her first semester, that's that; it will be the first of a long progression. She knows it, and so will they. They won't let her go on this way forever. Without the degree—she closes her eyes.

She knows this feeling. She hasn't lost her hold for sure yet; she can still fight, could still stay up all night and maybe pass her exam. It probably wouldn't be enough. Each minute she puts the choice off is a little less to be gained by trying. The fear of it kept her outside in the rain for two hours, and the two hours made the fear far worse. She knows that.

It's too late already, she thinks, her eyes on the mirror she has not touched. The best chance she ever had to start everything over and she's spoiled it so soon, so soon, the same way she always has. She looks at the mirror and through the mirror to the bottles that wait quietly inside, and she looks at her bare feet, numb from the cold, and she thinks: I don't know how to beat this.

April Fool

Robert Wallace

At first I miss the torn note—taped to the front door at navel level—until it flaps in the breeze like a lost page. Before removing it, I bend at the waist and while holding the bottom of the unlined paper with my index finger and thumb, read the bold faced words: DO NOT ENTER: MURDER IN PROGRESS. I freeze.

This is my wife's house, our house.

Barbara has not worked since we "lost" the baby. The baby's room remains unchanged, right down to the teddy bear border appliquéd at the top of the walls. During the day, while at work, I imagine Barbara reclining on the carpet, gazing at the bears sitting on the blocks of letters. A, B, C, I imagine her whispering, and her eyes shuffle within their sockets.

On sleepless nights she'll enter the baby's room, leaving the lights off so she doesn't wake me. I hear her bare feet skip across the hardwood floor, the touch of her palm rubbing the walls, a severe sigh when she stops.

"Are you all right?" I ask when she returns.

"It's like someone losing a limb. I still hear her."

Sometimes I catch her going through the baby's clothes. Taking them out of the drawers, she unfolds the pink and yellow dresses, the tiny white booties, lace and bows circling the ankles.

"Just keeping things tidy," she might say

"Tidy away," I say, biting my lip.

I try the door, but it's locked.

Because for years now I haven't carried house keys since Barbara always lets me in, I rush around to the side of the house. Along the way I wad the note and shove it in the front pocket of my pants.

Through the sliding glass door I see her spread out on the sofa, a bare leg protruding out of her gathered robe. Perched upon her chest is a red stained kitchen knife. Lifting a wrought iron chair, I swing it into the patio door. At the point of impact a giant starburst—shiny and silver and pointy all around—explodes inside the glass, sending spider-like cracks from the epicenter, and a deep fissure from one corner nearly to the other.

But the glass remains intact.

For days after, it is the sound of the crack widening and deepening that I remember the most. The sound of inevitability. How once the jagged line reaches the top, it pauses, then separates, causing one half to fall into the house. The other half, crashing before my feet, shatters into pieces. Years later I still find slivers in the sand between the bricks.

I enter the house, noticing that everything in the room is how I left it this morning, including a full cup of black coffee softly placed on the cherry end table. My hard leather shoes grind shards of glass into the wood floor. Suddenly I feel that my life—already splintered and moving away from me like a vision—is about to become an unfinished apology.

And that's when Barbara, after unflinchingly removing the knife, bolts upright. "Did you have a good day, Dear," she says, laughing.

"What the—!" I stop, for I find myself dumbstruck in the presence of her trickery.

"It was hidden here," she says, pointing between her arm and body. And then she takes the knife and holds it above her cocked head, licks the dripping ketchup, and I watch the long tip of her tongue curl at the end.

I look down at the floor and see how the bits of glass reflect the light from the lamp like a pool of water shimmering under the sun, and while fingering the note in my pocket, think: *So it has come to this.*

Common Ground

Annie McGreevy

Ian and I are alike in a number of ways that get us into trouble on our own and with each other all the time. We both have shaky relationships with the alien virtue know as self-control to some, boredom to others. We are the others.

Our respective weaknesses with this discipline have led to him cutting ten inches off of my hair when I only asked him for a trim, me introducing him to my friends from work as my little brother who is "just about to graduate high school," and him convincing everyone at my office holiday party that he was first Russian, then South African, then somehow managing to offend just about everybody.

These incidents mostly take place after we've spent hour upon hour at our favorite bar downtown, called Common Ground—with the exception of the hair-cutting, which happened in his bathroom after I had a bad day at work and a half a bottle of rum. Common Ground is a small, crowded bar with no cover charge, two-dollar beers and an entertaining mix of bike messengers and Venezuelan ex-patriots.

We were sitting there with a group of friends last Friday night when Miguel, who is both Venezuelan and a bike messenger, asked about Ian's bandaged-up hand. Ian just looked at me and barked like a dog.

It was so loud in the bar that I had to lean in close to Miguel. "Last night on the cab ride home, there were so many of us that Ian and I had to ride up front together. I had my arm out the window to make more room and he kept reaching over me, trying to roll the window up so I'd have to bring my arm in—you know, just trying to annoy me and make us even more cramped." Miguel smiled. He was really listening intently. If Ian hadn't have been there, looking all sad and little-boyish, I would have told

Miguel how Ian had been annoying me all night—he hadn't been buying his share of rounds, but taking advantage of everyone else who had been, and made fun of the nice man at the bar who asked for my number.

"So anyway, I took his hand off the window control and brought it up to my face." I laughed and Ian looked away.

That night in the cab was the most shocked I had ever seen Ian and the only time I saw him speechless. I guess he thought I was going to kiss him or something. I loved that look on his face—it made me feel like I had just won something.

"Then I bit down so hard on his finger that it bled all over the cab driver—'Mazungus'! He yelled at us. 'Get out!'—and there we were, on the curb with only $3.17 between us."

Miguel and some others within earshot cracked up. Miguel likes me, and we knew each other long before Ian moved into our neighborhood, and Ian understands this. Miguel winked at me and bought another round for everyone and Ian put his hand on his lap underneath the table.

At this point I've sort of accepted that these incidents between me and Ian. He won't stop, and I won't either. We may apologize later, but we'll never stop. For the same reason that we both cheated in junior high (fun) and also both cheat on anybody who is unlucky enough to stick around long enough to be called boyfriend or girlfriend (boredom, lack of self-control), I know that we both feel deep down somewhere that we have met our match.

Not our soul mate or anything like that. The way I feel about Ian reminds me of my old friend Ann Touchette—a girl who lived a few blocks away from me growing up. Her parents were from France and she had even been born there. We were connected at the hip for most of pre-adolescence, but in high school when we would find ourselves viciously competing for the same boys and leads in school plays, we were best friends one day and worst enemies the next. Looking back now, it's like we both raced to the front of the line to get to a roller coaster that only had one seat left in the front. This was the place we both wanted to be—where the wind blew through your hair, everybody else heard your scream first as you raced down the hill, and a camera took the picture of you having so much fun.

I'm sure someday, I'll have plenty of reasons to hate Ian, plenty of problems in my life to blame on him. But for now, I just enjoy watching him: the way he sighs when he tries to pick up change with his left hand with his ring and pinkie fingers (since his pointer and middle fingers are taped together), how he shoves his bandaged hand behind his back when he goes up to the bar for a drink, and, most of all, how silly he looks when he tries to smoke, paranoid that the white gauzy blanket is going to catch fire.

That night, Ian went home early, moody and tired. Our other friends left alone or in groups, and Miguel offered to walk me home after last call. He paid for my drinks, even after I pleaded for him not to. He just smiled his nice Miguel smile and offered me his jacket. It was August, when walking through Washington DC at night is like walking through a sauna, but that's the way he is: if he has a jacket, he offers it to a lady, even a lady that bites people.

We were almost to my house when he started asking me about Ian, fishing around. Miguel has had a crush on me for as long as I can remember. I was drunk and tired enough to just come out and give him answers to all the questions he was dancing around: "No. And no," I said and smiled as I spun inside the gate to my little yard, leaving Miguel on the other side.

He slowed down and looked sort of sad as he tossed his jacket over his shoulder. But then he laughed and we said goodnight. I sat on the porch and smoked the last cigarette in my pack. I was just about to go in when Miguel came trotting back down the street and stopped in front of my fence. "Hey," he said, panting a little. "I gotta know. If you don't like him, and there's nothing going on…then why did you do it?"

"Do what?" I asked. The final embers of the cigarette had already turned to ash on the step between my feet. I had forgotten all about Ian and his finger. I was thinking about Ann—if she still knew how to turn on her French accent when it would get her something, if she was married yet. I wondered if she still had blond hair, or if it had darkened with age, like mine had.

"You know," Miguel said sheepishly. "Bite him. Bite his finger last week. In the cab?"

"Oh, that!" I laughed and stood up. "I don't know," I said. "I just wanted to see what he tasted like." I turned around and walked up to my door and Miguel stood there outside my gate like he was waiting, patiently, as he is always willing to do, on a long line. The opposite of Ian, Ann, and me, who refuse to wait behind others.

I'm In Love With G.P. Lainsbury

Tanya Clary-Vandergaag

... then again, I am prone to notorious exaggeration (a trait G.P Lainsbury has reassured me I use simply because I lack knowledge, which apparently hinders my ability to write anything of value), but at least I have a crush on him. I can say that I definitely Have a Thing for him.

What's weird is that I've known G.P. Lainsbury for over four years and in those four years have only enjoyed him as the subject of insulting jokes to my girlfriends, the ones of "low academic and social standing". But lately I'm finding his utter condescension, his blatant repugnance for "my type" makes me as horny as a goddamn apple.

I have always only merely tolerated G.P. Lainsbury. Actually, we hardly tolerate each other—he barely, and often not even, tolerates my utmost disregard for his obvious "superior education" and arrogant intellectual abilities. Tolerating me is being generous. I, on the other hand, only just barely accept the fact that every single sentence he speaks is laden with criticisms of all the well-functioning, well-adjusted people of society. Multiply that by his belief, contrary to all evidence, that he really is a very cool guy, which is absurdly false, and you can see why I mostly just detest him.

But something has changed. Lately I have found myself going to Dr. Lainsbury's office with half-hearted attempts at articles, waiting for him to reprimand me for my "substandard work." He actually says "substandard" too, using the term frequently. It's a word that most conscientious, socially astute people safely steer away from, simply because it's burdened with such obvious arrogance. But not G.P. Lainsbury. What is really pathetic is that I can feel my nipples rise and harden with the simple purr of the word "substandard," and his forthright contempt for my "rhetoric." After looking over my "second-rate" writing, with every stroke and scribble of his ever-sharp, 0.5 mm Staedtler pencil, I get weaker and weaker. Just the thought of it makes me want to go back home and underline all my references, make short dashes instead of long ones—I wonder if he'd spank me if I misquoted Kafka? Christ, I get randy just thinking about his plastic-covered library of published reviews.

So, sure enough, as the perfectly weighted pencil crosses out my words, gutting my work like an ultra-hyper liposuction surgeon, I can't stop myself from picturing his cock, very similar, I bet, to the long, thin pencil in his hand. I am sure it would be lengthy, exact and very, very sharp. As he turns my pages, I squirm just watching his keyboard-flattened fingers work away.

You see, my middle-class, mediocre—no, my "substandard" education, along with my "truck-stop waitress refining school education," makes him snicker with contempt. Sadly, it's the snide look on his face as I confess to him that I took remedial math in high school that makes me so horny. He is convinced I have fucked my way to, what and where, I don't know, but to somewhere, because pretty girls like me always fuck their way through life—it's the "curse of the beautiful" that he hopes I will confess to one day. I find myself desperately trying to recall a pathetically demoralizing experience with some aging, illiterate boss who took advantage of my complete idiocy. What's sick is that I really really want it to be true, just so I can tell him some sorry tale of degradation due to my feeble-mindedness, just so I could watch his smug face sneer at his wise perception. If only I had one little story, dammit.

Bottom line is this—I am quite convinced that for all the university graduate seminars he has attended, rubbing CV's with all the highly acclaimed wanna-be's of the literary world, all the academic conferences he has lectured at, on his well-researched topics, I am quite certain, beyond doubt, that he has never ever laid his miserable white collar hands on an ass like mine before. I admit it, that's about as trashy as it gets, and I know it.

But, now, when I walk into his office and I give Dr. Lainsbury my work, I've stopped spell-checking completely, started using words completely out of context. If only he would just reach over and suck on my nipples while crooning "the derivation of that word is significant, even if your lack of knowledge does not allow you the ability to use it in its proper form." Instantly, as he begins his monologue on my numerous unlettered blunders, my imagination goes off on all sorts of tangents and I start to picture myself straddling the armrests of his recently purchased Basics Executive 399 series navy and gray leather computer recliner and I cannot see past the his tongue moving while he berates me: "the Greek prefix transmitted via the Latin is … " I start to sweat, swear to god.

As he goes on and on, on and on it goes—the porno movie in my head. I start to picture myself sitting bare-assed on his desk, my red painted toenails glaringly out of place in his retro-communistic décor, my feet on his narrow shoulders. He turns another page and I see myself leaning my head against his computer monitor, the picture of Henry Miller staring down at me from his screen saver, there I am, and all I am asking for are some Latin terms for fuck me harder.

As I leave, I press my wounded writing tight against my chest. I always turn back around. I can't help it. See, as low and pathetic as he thinks I am, it never fails that the brilliant Doctor can never resist catching a glance of my trailer-trash-cultivated ass, and at that moment I can feel how desperately he would like to have my hacked up article back in his hands.

SpringFest Encounter

Greg Lilly

I saw her looking at an art nouveau vase. Her delicate hands glided across the smooth ceramic, tracing the etched pink arches on the sides of a lime rectangle. I swear I heard angels sing when she glanced in my direction and smiled.

The downtown streets of Charlotte filled with people in shorts, t-shirts, and sunglasses; a big change from the usual starched Friday afternoons. SpringFest, an annual rite of the season, had started. Vendor tents displaying everything from pottery to funnel cakes lined Tryon Street.

I cut out of the bank early to meet some friends at street level for a few beers and some people watching. After changing clothes in the bathroom, I emerged into the bright sunshine and saw Clyde and Austin waiting at the corner. Clyde, still wearing his dark blue business suit, looked like a teddy bear ready for a meeting—all business, no fun, until the beer starts flowing and he turns into Mr. Personality. As for Austin, he's our "babe bait." Good looking kid, but gay as they come and proud of it. Women are attracted to his innocent look—doe eyed and prettier than a lot of girls I've dated. Austin will strike up a conversation with a woman and then introduce us to her. He hooks her; all we have to do is reel her in. So, there we stood like the Three Stooges waiting for something to happen.

"Let's get a beer, boys." I punched Clyde in his starched cotton covered gut. I found the beer truck easily by the tangy smell of cold Budweiser on hot concrete. The girl taking money flirted with Austin. I turned to Clyde and winked, a babe bonanza. Personally, I never had a hard time meeting women; it's Clyde who needs the help.

After some discussion on what to do next, we split up. Clyde and Austin followed the lure of hickory smoke billowing from the grills at the "Taste of Charlotte" tents. I checked out the artists' displays near a stage where beach music echoed off the surrounding buildings. That's when I saw her looking at some pottery. Had she really smiled at me?

A group of laughing teenage girls cut me off as I tried to make my way to the pottery tent. When I walked in, she was gone. Lost: blonde and blue-eyed, like the ideal woman of my childhood, Olivia Newton-John. The faint scent of a floral perfume lingered. I closed my eyes, trying to burn the fragrance into my memory.

I frantically searched each tent one after the other. Couples with strollers slowed me down.

A blonde flash entered a goose-themed craft tent. Would I really want a woman who liked this type of stuff? What if her idea of a wonderful vacation is Myrtle Beach? What if she's a Republican? What would she teach our kids? Would she wear Laura Ashley clothes and get frumpy? I wanted her to make heads turn when we walked by; to be a virgin when I finally convince her I'm Mr. Right and we spend the weekend in a mountain cabin; to know how to please me like no woman ever has in spite of being a virgin; to love my friends; to like football, fishing, theater, pasta, and my dog Ralph; to have her own career (making slightly less than me); to be my best friend. Basically, I wanted her to be a female version of me.

A sudden cool breeze swirled the scent of lavender around me. Her perfume, Olivia had to be close. A sparkle of gold shimmered in the tree filtered sunlight near the sidewalk. There she was, scraping the remnants of a chilidog off the bottom of her sandal onto the curb. How dainty she looked. Her face was filled with cool determination for the task at hand.

My heart beat faster. What would I say? The next few moments would determine my happiness for the rest of my life. I decided to offer my help with her current dilemma.

With one hand on a Bradford Pear and the other holding her lovely hair out of those Carolina blue eyes, she raked her sandal on the curb. My head began to spin. I managed to say: "Can I help you with that?" I gestured toward the problem sandal.

"Them God damn kids," she huffed "Just throw their trash down here anywhere. I just bought these shoes at the Wal-Mart. You didn't see who did this, did you? I'd like to rub his nose in this shit. Damn, damn, damn." She searched the surrounding crowd for the culprit, scratched her ass, and then continued to scrape the sandal.

Her wide feet, highlighted by chipped pink nail polish, packed the cherry red sandals. My head spun so fast I almost lost my balance. My gaze went back up, looking for something stable and soothing to steady my mind. Somehow during her struggle with the offending chilidog, she became partially free of her strapless bra. Her sundress now had one free wheeling breast and one constrained. The situation reminded me of a Georgia O'Keefe painting: I wanted to look away, but the unexpected eroticism spellbound me.

She interrupted my thoughts. "God, I need a beer. If you want to help, stop gawking and get me a beer." She picked the last stubborn scraps off with a twig. "Damn, I need a cigarette, got one?"

What had I been thinking?

"You stay right there. I'll get that beer and a napkin for your sandal."

I found Clyde and Austin walking down the street, and I jogged up to them. "The Antichrist is here disguised as a woman in sandals." I made Austin change shirts with me so if she saw me again, she might not recognize me. We headed back into the crowd for more babe cruising. This time, I would be more careful.

That's when I saw her...

Good Women

Lisa Selin Davis

I am not now nor will I ever be a good woman. I am not instantly charmed by children, nor polite when asking if anyone is using this chair. I do not smile regularly, or without deciding on it first.

I hate blondes, and happy women, and husbands parading their miniature versions like expensive toys with remote controls.

But an old man with a cat on a leash, a sharp-tongued, balding, angry old man with his drooling, furious feline refusing to follow, that will make me shine. An old man, formerly a sailor, in faded patriotic stripes, soaked to the collarbone in mid-August humidity, unyielding in his commands to the cat, and the dogged cat, unamused by puns, hissing, his parched tongue loose and waving like a flag: this pair, they will make me happy.

The man hates children, too. He loves it when the youngsters are fascinated by his little calico Mickey, when they crawl up to him, chubby paws reaching out to pet and the thing slaps its fangs on pink flesh. The man shrugs his shoulders deliciously as the contented cat collapses on macadam for his afternoon nap.

What is wrong with her, the other women wonder, that she is amused by the misfortunes of others and not touched by tiny successes? Surely it is jealously that twists her matronly callings into curses?

Girls, I can't broil a thing. I'll never be a good wife.

I am not a good woman, not generous save for the one big decision I've yet to make: to make, not to make, another me.

Become Thin and Attractive

Oz Spies

Start with your friends. Talk about who has the right bangs, whose mother insists on horribly practical clothes, like Kayla who still wears jeans with zippers on the ankles. Change the subject when Kim tells Sarah that she was at your house last night when your mom found some note from a woman in your dad's briefcase and threw a pan of lasagna at him. Throw notes across Social Studies class about how Matt broke up with Kayla because of her fat butt. Read your friends' techniques to become model-thin: laxatives, vinegar on everything. Practice writing your name with an "i"—Ami—because it's more exotic that way, like Cindy Crawford's mole.

Go to Matt's house after school with Mackenzie. Have an Altoid as you walk into the basement. Notice the lights are dim. Let Andy Cooper lead you to the corner. Sit on Andy's lap when he tells you to, and kiss him. Be proud to be pretty enough to make out with an eighth grader. Do not let him put his tongue into your mouth. Change your mind, but do not let him put his hands under your shirt. Gasp when you see the clock blinking 4:45; run home.

Lie in bed at night and pinch your skin, no, your fat. Worry that Andy felt it. Worry that it's 11:42 and your father's at work. In the next month, lose ten pounds. Smile when Andy says you're hot. Buy belts to cinch your jeans. Forget to bring lunch to school and make out with Andy behind the backstop instead.

Run. Burn calories. Do thirteen sets of thirteen sit-ups. Go into your father's closet and count fourteen gray suits and five black suits. Eat five carrots for dinner, chewing each bite twenty five times. Try not to think about food. Flip on the television and watch thin sitcom girls with beautiful hollow cheeks. Remember the apple pie. Sit on the kitchen floor and scoop pie up with your fingers; gulp it down. Feel your stomach bloat and sticky cinnamon cling to your chin. Weigh yourself and realize you've gained three pounds since morning. Slump down on the cool tile, over the toilet, and make yourself throw up until only water's left. Feel clean, empty. Take a shower, clean the kitchen, go to bed.

Ignore Sarah and Kim when they say you're getting too skinny and it's really kind of gross. Take deep breaths when you get light headed. Cry when Andy breaks up with you because you're weird. Cry harder when you see him kissing Mackenzie behind the backstop.

Go to Walgreen's and wander through the makeup aisle. See the clerk at the front helping a man wearing tight plaid pants; dash to the dietary products section. Slip extra-strength laxatives in your pocket. Buy a container of peach lipstick. Mumble when the clerk tells you to have a nice day and race out. Toss the ugly lipstick and pop three laxatives.

Do jumping jacks in the bathroom. Write Andy a note about Mackenzie's bad habits: zit popping, snoring. Tell him about the time Mackenzie laughed so hard when you toilet papered Jim's house that she peed her pants and had to borrow a pair of your jeans, which were too tight on her. Don't sign the note. Deny everything when your old friends ask.

Wear winter clothes when everyone else starts wearing shorts because you can't stop shivering. Tell your mother you're fine when she says she's worried. Pretend you can't hear your friends call you skeleton girl during passing period. Dream about thick homemade bread, enchiladas, and Snickers. Punish yourself with extra laps around the block. Jog by Kim's house, because you know she's having a slumber party. See Mackenzie and Sarah's bikes in the driveway. Let the air out of their tires, then run home.

Worry your father's stuff is disappearing: the closet has no black suits, and only five gray. Scream how important it is that you talk to your father when his secretary tells you that he's on a business trip so he can't take your call but you can leave a voice mail, sweetie. Attempt to reunite your parents by giving them an opportunity to talk without access to food to throw. Remember how well it worked for Hayley Mills; tell your parents it's parent-teacher night. Pretend to be asleep when they come home after a half an hour, so that you won't get yelled at because it wasn't parent-teacher night and the school was dark and locked up. Listen to them come upstairs, then to your father's heavy footsteps going back down alone.

Count your sips of water. Profess that everything is fine when your mother tells you how concerned she is because you're skin and bones. Tell her it's the start of a growth spurt: you're that age. Leave for school. Hide behind the backstop, then walk back home after your mother's left for work. Pace the living room while you watch TV because Sarah once told you that you burn fewer calories watching TV than sleeping. Go for a run and slump down on the sidewalk mid-stride; pass out.

Smile at your mother and father when you wake up in the hospital, a thick wad of tape keeping the IV in your arm. Bring your hands, each holding one of your parents' hands, together on your stomach, so all four hands meet. Cough when your mother asks why you haven't been eating and your father snaps at her to stop badgering you. Feel your limbs drain as you follow your mother's gaze down to her hand; try not to notice the thin strip of pale skin on her ring finger.

Drop their hands and think about the kickboxing class you're going to take the minute you get out of the hospital to work off the sugar in the IV, and how jealous your friends will be of your perfect body.

The Red Hat

Janis Mitchell

There is a girl with a red hat, outrageous sashay, quirky twist of a ponytail, regenerated sophistication barely realized as she storms past a character waiting for the tram. Do you see her? Do people notice a girl like that? Do eyes travel from the words of a page, a newspaper perhaps, letters to hips, following. How can you miss an inspiration, a self-generated tornado, a girl with a red hat, a red-lipped smile, and red-heeled shoes to match?

A character, a boy, sees.

He watches her as the tram approaches; she glides from curb to step to tram, sneaking through all those eyes. As the double door slides shut, groaning, a separation of his and her self, she turns and smiles directly at him. She is gently kissing a cherry at her lips. She offers him some fruit from the little paper bag she balances open on one hand.

Then she turns away to the back of the tram, floating through the narrow strip between standing passengers, men keeping tight grips on steel poles. All the while the boy sees and the girl forgets.

He wonders what person she is, could be.

The tram door jerks open a second time.

The boy approaches the girl. "Hello friend," he says.

She glances at him non-committal

"Do I know you?" she asks: chilly welcome from a girl who understands how to play.

"You offered me fruit," he smiles.

"Did I?" she sighs, steals a quick glance at her reflection in the window.

"I'll take it now," he says, simply.

The girl considers and holds out the bag; it is in her hand, crumpled still. The boy reaches and there is an exchange.

"So where do you go?" she questions.

"I'm following you."

The girl disguises an approving grin as it creeps along, claiming her face from forehead to dimpled chin.

"Do you mind?"

"Yes. Of course." (But she doesn't.) "You can't just follow me."

"Why not? I'm going to believe only in you."

"You have no right to choose me in a crowd." Picture hands on jutting hips.

"You chose me," he says.

The girl notices this boy's opaque brown eyes, his Mediterranean skin, his left ear slightly bigger than the right. His gentle laugh and his concentrated gaze. "What do you do?" His mouth has a slight twitch.

"I stand," says the girl, "I make you question who you are. I'm a million different souls."

"An actor?" he guesses.

For the girl there is something near pleasure in the long silence she creates and, with the flick of a polished fingernail, ends. "Do you know the beginning of the streetcar was in the 1880's?"

"Yes." The boy did know. "Can I have your phone number?"

"No. What do you think, because we are talking now I should give you my number?"

"I want to see you again."

"But you see me now. Don't you think that is enough?"

"Yes," the boy begins, "I mean no ... " He ends as the girl laughs softly, accepting his confusion. "Did you notice that we have traveled in a circle?" stammers the boy. "We are back where we started." He looks out the window. He whispers, "Do you think we will ever get off this tram?"

"I think we'll keep spinning." She offers another cherry.

the kind of love they talk about in movies

Lisa Selin Davis

1.   In the end Eva Braun's main concern was her own beautiful corpse. Her husband (why did they marry like that, at the end? Was it for property, or tax purposes?) killed his own dog, fed Himmler's cyanide to sweet innocent Blondie—just to see—convinced as he was that his right hand man's treachery extended to weak poison.

2.   It seems they really loved each other.

3.   You keep cyanide in a jar, in a beaker is it? In a lance? Somewhere in your lab you are storing this powder, this power. You told me the inventory and I wanted to tug on you, bring some home, slip in under the cork, press it into a patty and grill it for me, would you? You know me well enough now to guess my final meal, chocolate and cheeseburgers and a mickey slipped in to save me.

4.   When Eva saw Adolph stooped over, she scolded him. He told her, You try standing upright with this many keys in your pocket.

5.   When I saw you with your shoulders back, I wanted to scold you. I stuck my hands in the scalloped chino holes from when you'd fallen off your motorcycle, but I could not bring you down.

6.   You work in a room with a letter and three numbers on the door. I shook the integers out of you. It took six weeks, and still I don't know where you are. I don't know what you do in there.

7.   In the end poison would not suffice, and they burned him beneath a polished cotton sheet. That was love, they really loved each other.

8.   Marry me, then kill me; that's all I want from you.

The Biggest Mistake

Lisa Selin Davis

Don't play in the street. Wipe your feet, there's white tile, don't you see it? Stop torturing the cat, the poor cat, your little brother. Come on over here and give your mother a hug, everything I do for you, what I've sacrificed.

Have you learned yet to speak? Were you born with any birthmarks, with Down Syndrome, with flippers for arms, with attached earlobes, with lupus, with luck? Would we have been that mother and son I saw every day climbing the city bus, the beautiful blond boy, the midget, and his mama with the perma-frown, circumnavigating a constant cloud of regret?

Why do I think you were a boy, when all the names I've had picked, names culled from childhood books and carefully reprinted in purple diaries, were girl names? How would I have called you, and where would we live now, here? The desert? The city? A suburb somewhere in between the coasts?

I played cards this week with a man who was not your father. I placed a five on the pile and he slapped down his Jack and guffawed. He said, "That was your biggest mistake," and earned two points.

Your father is rich now. He records sound, James Gandolfini and Edie Falco, captures their dialogue in tiny wireless microphones on the Asbury boardwalk. We're talking thousands every week. You and I could live in a sweet one-bedroom in Brooklyn, a good public school for you, two uncles and an aunt and four grandparents; we would have been all right. I'd paint your corner of the living room pumpkin, to make you hungry, paint the bathroom turquoise like the bottom of a pool.

I should never have let them clean you out, never have lost that gamble. Forgive me, would you? I should have let you grow.

The View From The Top

Julie Paul

It's my turn tonight. When it's his turn, with signals alongside his face, or a thumb grazing his left shoulder, Adam tells me from the stage who he wants and I set to work. I'm on tour with his band, as the Supportive Girlfriend, keeping his back rubbed, his gig shirts washed, the merch table well stocked. Last show she was a woman with salon dreads, in a silk bikini top: he goes for bouncy. I prefer the contained, internal dancers, their eyes closed, bodies allowing the music in but not letting it take over. I've chosen a woman in a white halter, criss-cross tie in the back, band around the neck. A single blue bead on a silver chain hangs close to her singing throat.

She's talking into the ear of an Australian guy with a shaved head, the folds of his scalp wrinkled and hairy, pushed like continental ridges over his occiput. He's like a piston to the rhythm when he dances solo, and when he's holding her, bent forward to tent her, I can, all too easily, picture them having sex. The intense five minutes, the vestigial hope on her face while he gets right to the snoring.

This is what you get.

The deal is that we do it during Karma Police. Adam's band does a wicked cover, and the audience always sings along. Every night, it's a new town, a different crowd, but still the same set, the same rules—and at least one woman on the floor wearing what we're looking for.

We do it and wait for the fallout. I say "we," but it's my hands that do it, no matter who makes the pick. We've had it all: anger, shock, screams, slaps, tears. Yet I escape the wrath with one finger, pointed in a certain direction, a look of surprise and empathy on my innocent face. We do it because it's like dropping a penny off the CN tower, like throwing a rock through a picture window, consequence-free. It's about giving into the itch of temptation. We do it because we can. And because, after two months on the road, I'm looking for diversions. Long live rock and roll, sure, but I might perish from boredom first.

The Australian leaves to take a piss and I make my move. I get up close to those dangling loops of the woman's bow, flapping like small wings that perk and relax with every move. Her shoulders roll and tip; her head agrees with the beat.

Adam signals the soundman with a wave, a point to the mike and an upward thrusting thumb. Translation: Bring up the vocals. Showtime.

Yes indeed. I give Adam my own sign. She's the one.

This is what you get, when you mess with us.

I grab the ends and with one quick tug, like the snap of a Christmas cracker the bow is gone and the latticework becomes sloppy, then disintegrates as the woman raises her arms to cheer the band on.

We're about to get feedback.

I'm ready for the reaction, for the all-at-once recognition that things are not as they were, the whirl around, the venom ready. Or, the incomprehension of the naive. I have my finger ready to be aimed at the man beside me, a shaggy-haired wild man who knows how to swear in Spanish. I've become a mistress of deflection.

But nothing happens. She's still dancing, raising her arms, head still saying yes, and after the cheering, the whistles, the final note, she's got only a flap of white poly-lycra hanging from her neck, the sides of her breasts fully aware of the bar, taking in all the sights and sounds. That shirt, hanging like a bib, strings like wind catchers, decorative fringes, nothing more. Like a sail waiting for the breath of a smoking god.

I've got Shaggy Boy in the line of my finger-fire, but when the woman turns around to see who did it, there's a mischievous grin on her face. I don't know what to do. This has never happened. I'm shocked into confusion.

And everyone's belting out: *For a minute there, I lost myself. I lost myseeeeeeelf.*

So before I can think I end up pointing my finger at myself

and then at my boyfriend, his shirt unbuttoned in the light show heat, a double shooting, and the woman gives Adam a look before she hoists the sail of her shirt for him, and Australia Man is coming back and the next song is building to the drum intro and once the band really starts giving it, she says to me, Would you mind giving me a hand?

Adam's watching us both carefully now. I shrug.

Okay, I say. A blush spreads through my body like a niacin flush.

We'll be right back, she says to the man from Down Under who gives me the once-over and I follow her unfettered torso as it weaves through the sweating bodies. And we go into one stall, close the door, and, criss-cross applesauce, ennui nowhere to be seen, we get the shiveries.

The Song Jimmy Used To Sing To Drown Out
The Sound Of The TV Coming From Next Door

Linda Mannheim

I remember the private eye shows we used to watch when we were kids where, one guy, usually a loner, got framed for murder or something, and he had to spend the rest of the show doing a song and dance, wiggling fast before they got him in the hole. He always got away from the cops just before the bullet cut his skin and had time to spare in order to knock apart the frame. After that, he'd confront the cops with nails between his teeth, holding rough torn boards and standing on the ground as if his foot was on the earth's belly and he was a victor somehow. Like those men you see who climb to the top of a mountain or make it to the North Pole. A haha in the end, a walk away, spit words between his teeth, go for a beer and who gives a damn. Damn. I would walk like him, walk like a man and keep my butt straight instead of wiggle.

"You've been walking that way to get me to follow you," Jimmy said, with a gulp.

But I followed him. Into the kitchen. Small of my back against the metal edge of the kitchen table, and Jimmy up against me in the jeans he has been wearing for three days, enough of a beard on his face so it hurts, his mouth hot and wet as the air outside.

When they came for him at first, they came asking like he was the biggest scum that ever walked the face of the earth. They had seen the movies too. White boys in ties trying to act tough. The big one, the pale guy shaped like a half-droop balloon with smooth black hair plastered close to his face, he moves in front of me in the doorway, and he says to me, "We can get you too for harboring a fugitive if you don't cooperate."

Jimmy once had a plan, once. When we were lying in bed, wrapped in each other in the dark, we watched a video, and you know that part where the little warning comes up, the FBI warning telling you about the copyright laws? Jimmy had a plan to rent every video from the store on a 168th street, then tape over the FBI warnings so the new one would read: "Warning: If the FBI comes to your house, make sure you contact a lawyer before you talk to them."

His tee shirt on my cheek was rough. I put my face in him breathing deep the smell of him, cotton, and sweat. He said, "I am going under now. I am going under." He goes. I look out. See the street, the brick wall, the other buildings. And people hanging out. And the writing on the wall. The summer so hot and crowded, I don't know where there is for him to go. Maybe under's the only place to be, place where there's space.

I think: under. Under. Like the subway at night. Late at night, when it's empty. Everyone's too scared to be down there. Or maybe at Highbridge Pool. Daytime, so many bodies in that pool, ain't no place to swim. You go there at night though, climb the wall, get to the top, sit there with a little something to drink, legs swinging. You find your place. Deep, cool water. Cool, when the night's so thick and hot, you wanna cut it. You take the bridge in your hand like knife and slice the night so steam rises and you wish you could save that for winter when you're walking your little apartment, cold, hugging in your coat. Gas stove on, and you hope the flame doesn't die out.

"Search the place, men." He flashes the search warrant.

I imagine it all, me and Jimmy, and our life like a cotton sheet stretched taut, then the silver of a knife points through. I watch the tear. The dresser drawers dumped, couch cushions pulled apart, everything undone. Oh Madre, I just got done cleaning up. After the goddamned day, the type type type. "Do you think you could get us a cup of coffee, laugh at my jokes, make my ego big?"

"You can be you or you can be them," Jimmy said, his big hand against my skinny arm. "It's up to you. When you're being them, I can see you shutting off. It's like a car, Elena. They turn the key and there's no motion anymore."

Standing here, frozen, I follow him up to the roof and they think I'm staying still, scared. Look south. You can see almost all of the city from here, but not everything. Look below Harlem, where the buildings start to get tall; The Chrysler Building (that's my favorite), The Empire State (where suicides leave holes the size of their bodies in the cars below), and hidden in the spiky towers, down near the Brooklyn Bridge, FBI headquarters, where they say his bomb went boom.

I want them to finish dumping. Finish dumping. Do these fuckers have to pay for anything that they break? Hey, you break it you buy it, boys. Get off my fucking life. "Now, if you agree to cooperate with us (agree to cooperate—kind of redundant?), we can assure you (they should be speaking in chorus), you will receive every benefit a cooperative witness is due."

And what benefits are those, balloon face? You'll iron my clothes, pick me up by car, make sure dinner's ready when I get home at night? You want me to spill the beans now or wait 'til I get a lawyer?

"Like I said, this could be one big mess for you. You could be in for a long, long time if you make the wrong choice."

I turn from him. There's a young one looking like he's ready to swallow me whole, licking his lips. Tonight, he's going back to Queens, back to his wife, the door he just refinished that his kids put Wacky Packages stickers on, and he'll try to tear it off. But right now, he's watching, shifting where he stands from foot to foot, waiting for instructions.

I put my hands on the cold radiator, chip off its silver paint. The night rises hot and ripe and dirty and clear midnight blue at the same time. Traffic rushes like the river, and music comes up from the shore. Everyone's outside watching another car pull up, blue lights violent as they hit the buildings now.

Save some room for me, Jimmy. I know you're out there.

SugarTime, When the Livin' Was

Ariana-Sophia Kartsonis

Billy Boyd, radio light & sweet-talk. I was seventeen and a half and Billy the boy a girl never forgives. Perry Como instructed: Catch a falling star, put it in your pocket, save it for a rainy day. I thought he meant Billy—thought he meant save him.

Elvis playing it spare that year. One word & that word was Don't. I should've listened to Elvis. The Silhouettes sang *Get a Job*. I was made for one thing.

My calling, surely, was to be the fourth McGuire Sister. Only I was born Italian, an only child, tone-deaf. Pitchless as armless boys dreaming baseball diamonds, their wooden bats cracking through summer skies.

Sugar in the mornin'. Sugar in the evenin'. Sugar at supper-time. Honey in the mornin' and so on until So don't you roam. (Billy B.) and be my little honeycomb.

All that glucose would gum up the whistle-cleanest of hearts. Billy's heart was lots of things, lost mostly. But clean?—as clean as a public toilet in old Bombay.

The night I left I left with these things: all the McGuire girls' lyrics plus Billy Boyd's baby inside me, seventy dollars of babysit-ting money, Billy's class-ring stolen from the ashtray of his aqua Impala that last night—Gigi playing the Star-vu Drive-In (which I hear starve you or Starve U-university because I learned lifetimes about hunger & absence that night). I learned Billy was as empty as I was full (&fool too), I'd never be a radio-star but I sang any-way as the last lights of town lost themselves to my rear-view—singing for two girls or four or more dotting every high-way between there & where I'd arrive.

Sky of Diamonds

Sally Haxthow

Here comes another one. Wants to talk to me, she says. Yeah, well who don't? One day it's a film student making a documentary for class, next day it's a policeman, new to the streets, gonna change the world one hooker at a time. Today it's a pretty young thing wants to profile our short -skirted asses on her news show.

I'd like to talk to you sweetheart, sure would like to help out with your career and all, but I need a fix so bad my hair is sweating yesterday's sweat; my teeth are falling outta my head over here so if you'd excuse me, today is not a good day. Wouldn't want to vomit on your Gucci, hoochie, give me a smoochie shoes. Click, click, click on the pavement she's fast. All style and grace and sweet smelling somethin' or other that ain't never touched the likes of my body. Her voice like crisp, clean water, and my mouth as dry as a desert.

But here comes JJ, and I know he's got my fix. He slithers by, green eyes like a snake, and it's in the breast pocket of my tiny denim jacket, beating hard against my heart. But still here's newsy girl, pretty in pink, in my face.

You're cuttin' into my business, I tell her. You want me to talk, you gotta buy my time, same as anybody else. Ain't no charity on this street sweetheart. Traffic gets a bit slow when the news cameras are out if you know what I'm sayin'. Boy, am I surprised when she pulls out a twenty. Just like that, twenty bucks. And all I gotta do is answer a few questions. But her questions are dull and I tell her so. You want some news, I ask her, you wanna give the audience what they're really lookin' for? I tell you what—you get the heck out of here and you let me get my fix and then you come back and we finish this. Will I shoot up on camera? Hell, I don't care, just shove off for god's sake, cause I got things I need to do.

So I got stuff in my pocket and I'm in my alley, fast, and I'm so hungry for it I don't care that newsy girl's heels are click, click, clicking behind me and I don't care if the camera light is hot light on my face, skin so tight it's about to rip. Newsy girl looks scared, and excited, and now she says maybe we shouldn't do this. But I know she doesn't really mean it. Last thing I see is her diamond earrings sparkling in the camera light, floating orbs like stars shining down on me and I can feel the hot, liquid life enter me and consume me and pretty in pink newsy girl ain't never had an orgasm as good as this and she knows it and I know it and now the camera knows it too.

Recipe For Sedition

Liesl Jobson

THE IMPOTENCE OF HE-WHO-SIGHS

At sundown, S'Khalo watches the white man's tractor return to the barn. Heavy clouds on the reddened horizon threaten a thunderstorm. Bees buzz forlornly in the yellow Acacias, intensifying his despair.

The swarthy Swazi cowherd passes behind S'Khalo, humming a suspicious tune. With a long strong stride, he gathers the animals into the thorny kraal then twists the wire latch. He stops in front of S'Khalo, quits his musical rendition, and, as he does each evening, sneers at the feeble fold in the old man's lap.

Once the cattle are lowing, Alpha Centauri mounts the sky, bright and hopeful. S'Khalo pretends to sleep. His youngest, prettiest wife slips out of the hut. S'Khalo groans in sorrow, stuffing his ears against the moans whispering and rising beyond.

Before dawn has turned the night with its promise, his youngest, prettiest wife returns with dew-wet feet and straw-speckled hair. He stares at her sleeping form sprawled on her sleeping mat and watches the light catch on the golden stalks nestling in her tight black curls.

At dawn, S'Khalo watches the white man's wife leave the barn. Soon the cowherd sneaks out humming a suspicious tune. S'Khalo remembers how desire once felt and curses the day he was named S'Khalo, which means "He-who-sighs."

THE LUCK OF HE-WHO-ROAMS

When Zulane left the Swazi Correctional Services in Mbabane, he wanted to go where murderous husbands and avenging fathers would not find him. He wished to avoid miniature versions of his own flat nose and black eyes complaining of hunger. Most of all he wished to avoid a re-arrest for failing to pay maintenance to the numerous wives who always managed to track him down with their endless court orders.

At night, he wandered southeast through the Ezulwini Valley, crossed the border and meandered along the N2 to Hluhluwe. By day, he lay in ditches, which he first cleared of the snakes that slept in the hot sun.

By the time he crossed the white man's farm he had been roving for ten days. The fragrance of roasting chicken assaulted him so that he could hardly stand to greet the girl who lingered over a cooking pot and the grandfather who gestured him to sit.

"Wife, bring this weary traveler beer," he ordered.

"Is there work in town?" Zulane asked.

"The farmer needs a cowherd . . ."

The young girl lifted her full breasts as she placed the frothy brew beside the handsome stranger. She put a steaming plate in his hand and licked her lips.

Looking at her moist pink tongue, Zulane felt for the foil-wrapped prison issue condom in his pocket and blessed the destiny of his name. He thanked the luck of "He-who-roams."

RECIPE FOR SEDITION

<u>Ingredients</u>
Several million HIV/AIDS positive men and women
Aging impotent husband
Swarthy Swazi cowherd
Light white farmer
Nubile Zulu maiden
Faithless white woman
One laundry
Pair of khaki shorts
One iron
One gun

Method:

First, reveal raw frailty of old man. Undress slowly on wedding night; rub his member until your arms are about to fall off. Scorn his impotence and say it is your constitutional right to have and to hold a working gun. Slip into the night while he pretends to sleep.

Secondly, admire musculature and prowess of swarthy boy. Look alluringly over cooking pot at his hunger and promise sweet and tender meat. At this stage, question whether Mr. Cowherd will wear a condom. If he refuses, refuse him too. Watch him battle his manly prerogative to consume his lust flesh-on-flesh. Once he concedes to wear the condom, disclose that you no longer desire him. Leave before resolution.

Thirdly, while on laundry duty the following morning, iron khaki shorts of light white man. When he enters the room, drop laundry item in surprise. Bend to retrieve, revealing ample thighs and insufficient underwear. Engage advances. Sigh happily.

Repeat third stage as necessary for a week or two, while observing Swazi's would-be seduction of faithless white woman.

Presentation:

Decorate with drollery; serve with savvy. Wonder aloud during pre-coital pillow talk about passionate cowherd's performance for farmer's wife.

Clean up tip:

Feign innocence when police investigate.

No Mulberry Trees; No Railroad Ties

Ariana-Sophia Kartsonis

No ties at all for Marmalade who cut them way back when the railroad went south and her words took the last train out before the whistle died out and Marmalade—sweet Marmalade was mute. Three years, seven months, two days plus morning since, and Marmalade is mute as thick pudding, as a stopped pocket watch, even now.

It wasn't all grief's fault about Marmalade. Though grief was an accomplice to all the bad weather. Whether she'd turned round and round those bushes with the old miner's daughter, Clementine, in the pretty day, pretty day of fall colored apple wine, purple leaf and burning orange air; and whether or not they fell down and kept falling until only Marmalade got back up, is no concern of grief's.

Now, the tracks have gone rusty and the train's stopped running. Two girls went spinning in the cider-wind of autumn; two girls went down in the fall field outside a once-upon-mining-town and one girl stood up.

Here's where memory came apart at the seams for Marmalade. Where everyone tells her there was no train, no severed girl, just some secret water and some foam and ruby lips gone chalky-grey. Marmalade crawled away from the waterside tracks and the crushed girl and the drowned girl and the sobbing miner and the way you don't forget that day just keep living and living it. The spinning to dizziness. The laughter. The blurry autumn every-where. The train whistle. The stumbling girl. The falling, the fall.

Touch death early and its lavender lips shush you some. There'll be more of the same. One minute and the world goes lopsided. One minute plus a scream and the bearing down and the crushed bones that aren't yours but feel achy when it rains and the rainwater reminds you. The rainwater that washes you in fall afternoon memories, washes over you and never makes you come clean. There are bathhouses forming even now in the quietest part of your mind. There are water-witchers out divining and they're closing in on you.

It's a cruel world, Marmalade's mama said, so sorry you had to see it, Baby. So sorry, truly am. But it keeps spinning this way, you may as well ready yourself. This world keeps spinning kind of drunk-like, kind of wobbly, spinning sad threads off its little wheel, weaves you a tapestry of sorry days and good days and they all tangle if they're too loose, unravel if you pull too tight, ache sometimes on a rainy day. And all the days sometimes they feel rainy. All the rainy days collect like seepage, underwater wells. Then the silly putty of your mind picks up pictures—funny paper people—and they stay until you stretch them out and warp them and then smear them all away. Dreadful sorry all the same.

The Ice Wizard

Marsha Francis

I make the ice-skaters fall. No really, I do. I don't push them down or anything, but it's true. I make them fall. Double Toe Loop, Triple Lutz, Triple Axel, it doesn't matter. I can sabotage them all. It starts with this feeling in the pit of my stomach, like just before the first drop of a roller coaster and then it happens. Bam! Ass on ice, every time.

My boyfriend says it's bullshit. Says there is no way that some cosmic force is coming together in my body to control the landings of ice skaters on a TV broadcast from Canada. Well, all I know is when I'm watching, the skaters land ass on ice when I say so.

Except Lipinski. I despise Lipinski. All teeth and hair, no artistry, not like Michelle. Michelle Kwan is an ice goddess. And I am directly responsible for her meteoric rise to the top of the skating world. For years I've supported her, making the competition fall left and right. Nicole Bobek, Maria Butyrskya, Irina Slutskaya. Yeah, that was me. But then came Tara Lipinski. A tiny bundle of pure energy capped by a mouthful of huge, gleaming, white teeth. She is my nemesis. I can't make her fall. Her feet stick to the ice on each landing and no amount of concentrated nudging on my part gets her ass any closer to the ice. And to rub it in, that little bitch celebrates each victory over me with a mocking grin that makes me wonder—whatever happened to Tonya Harding?

But, I know how she does it. Yes, I do. I'm on to her. See, last month, I got rink-side tickets to the Stars on Ice Tour. I figured I'd have a better shot at her if my cosmic force or whatever came at her from mere yards instead of over the airwaves. But I was wrong; even then I couldn't do it. It was like every time her feet left the ice there was some other cosmic force holding her firmly in perfect position for a smooth single bladed landing. And that's when it occurred to me. What if I'm not the only one? What if on the other side of the arena there is another ice wizard? Except, except that wizard keeps them up in the same way that I make them fall? So I started to look around for him. I studied each and every person rink-side, searching for him, and finally I found him!

Brian Boitano! He was standing just at the edge of the kiss and cry. And I knew it was him. I knew it was him because his beady little eyes narrowed every time Lipinski took a jump. And when her program was finished and she was taking her bows, that bastard turned, looked me straight in the eye—and winked.

Catch As Catch Can

Jason Nelson

Baseballs make fine friends. They understand social dynamic intricacies, and are practiced in the oddities of picking up chicks. I'm not saying they're very strong or even have arms. But each stitch represents a conquest, and even the scent of military might is a sex magnet. Sometimes when my baseball and I go out to the bars, she'll buy me a few drinks and lament the lack of available women. Then when it seems obvious she won't be getting lucky, she'll lean over and try to kiss me.

And although I might find her leathery skin and infinite curves physically appealing, I know that baseballs will never stray from their sexual orientation for long. Later that night she'll be angry, speeding at over ninety miles per hour down a snowy country road, and lose control, crashing into some fallow field. And then she'll call looking for a tow, because she's stuck and they don't make snow chains for baseballs.

Her Knees Are Weak

Diane E. Dees

Martha Crawford had gotten it on with just about every major Elvis impersonator in the country. Except, of course, that woman in Alabama, though Martha had certainly given the idea a passing thought. She decided against it, not because it was unnatural--what could be more unnatural than taking to bed a series of men with sideburns in glitter-decked jumpsuits?—but because the farther you got from the real thing, the less it was worth the trouble.

As president of the Gulf States Elvis the King Fan Club, Martha was able to get free tickets to see Elvis impersonation shows. She made two or three pilgrimages to Graceland a year and was given to stalking the streets of Tupelo, talking to strangers and searching for new tidbits about her idol. She limited her sexual encounters to the actual impersonators, however, because nothing turned her on more than an avatar of the King.

Martha's daddy had loved Elvis. Elvis was a real man, Daddy said. He was good to his mama, served his country, read the Bible and wasn't afraid to talk to or about the Lord. Daddy had loved Elvis the way women loved him, Martha thought, putting his picture in a frame, buying all of his records, never missing an Elvis movie. He had grown sideburns, which irritated the hell out of Martha's mother, but there was no talking him out of it. Daddy had slow-danced with Martha in the living room to "Are You Lonesome Tonight?" and ""Love Me Tender," and had held her tight and told her how pretty she was.

Martha was getting a little bored these days. Elvis impersonators had a limited bedroom repertoire and said things like "I got a hunk o' somethin' for you, honey," or "Wanna see my good luck charm?" She was a little tired of making peanut butter, banana and bacon sandwiches, too, and sometimes wished she could go out to dinner in a nice restaurant with a man who had normal hair and didn't sneer when he looked at her cleavage. But such was Martha's Elvis addiction that she wasn't sure she could let a non-Elvis touch her, much less do the wild thing with her. "TCB, baby!" she would shout, as soon as she was ready to go for it. Once, in Baton Rouge, a Las Vegas-era Elvis wasn't up to the task, leading Martha to point out that "the King really is dead."

Martha's only friends were fan club members, and try as they might, they couldn't really talk about anything that wasn't Elvis-related. Lisa Maria and Michael kept them going for a while, but once that was over, Martha became restless.

One night, she was watching TV and a newswoman began talking about the failed war against drugs. She showed that famous picture of Elvis and Nixon, and then commented that Nixon must have been living in a dream world if he hadn't known about Elvis's drug addiction. Daddy had never liked Nixon, so Martha hated him, too. Elvis's heart was pure, she knew that; people took advantage of him because he was a money machine. The doctors gave Elvis the drugs. He didn't know he was doing anything wrong.

The thought of Elvis as a drug addict began to haunt Martha. She didn't really mind fat Elvis; she had even voted for the fat Elvis stamp, just to show support. But if he really was an addict, then he must have felt high and desperate a lot of the time. She knew he missed his Mama. Gladys had meant everything to Elvis. Martha poured herself a bourbon and Coke and thought about Daddy lying in his casket, his sideburns shaved off because her mother had insisted on it. Martha had touched Daddy's hands, and they were cold, not like the hands that led her through their living room waltzes. Daddy would give her a little kiss on the cheek before she went out on a date, and he would pat her behind and whisper "You be careful, hon. You're Daddy's girl." Once, he kissed her on the mouth and she smelled beer and Old Spice and Daddy's sweat, and she felt weak, like her legs might not hold her up much longer.

Martha drank more bourbon, and the tears came. She could usually make them go away, but tonight, they had control of her. She got up and put on her Elvis love song collection, poured herself another drink and cried. She cried for Elvis, trying to find his way through life without Gladys, the only woman he had ever loved with all his heart. She cried for Daddy, dead from a heart attack--just like that—one afternoon before Martha had come home from school. Elvis sang "I Love You Because."

Martha, like most women, could cry only so much, and then she had to wash her face and apply teabags to her eyes. She decided to call the Elvis impersonator who lived at the edge of the next county, the one who had turned a pair of leather pants into a private floorshow for her in the casino lounge. He was young and firm, and he understood the moves, onstage and off. Maybe she could get him to have a drink with her, talk to her, take her to dinner.

Martha tried to picture the man without his sideburns. She tried to imagine him in a pair of khakis, shopping for groceries, or wearing pajamas and reading the newspaper. But how could she relate to a man in khakis? She changed the channel in her head and saw the black leather pants, the tight red shirt and the diamond rings. She fingered her gold chain and felt the TCB pendant between her breasts. She started to feel weak in the legs. In the background, the King sang "Baby, Let's Play House" as Martha picked up the phone.

Referred to Fondly As My Ex

Tracy J. Deobald

Revenge never tasted as sweet as the Chocolate Explosion Cheesecake I baked for my ex's wedding.

"What? Are you nuts, Woman?" Trudy G screeched when I told her. She vaulted onto my portable dishwasher and grabbed the cordless, pretending to dial. "White Jacket Hotel? We got a live one over here." Her pink-ribboned pigtails swung madly. "What kind of pms-ing, psycho-stupid woman makes a bloody wedding cake for her scum-sucking ex-fiancé?"

"Me." I grinned. I attached the blades to the hand mixer, feeling each one snick into place with a satisfying pop. "Dr. Phil says to forgive and then to get on with your life. So that is what I am going to do. A twenty-dollar cheesecake beats a two hundred dollar couch session. And we get to lick the beaters."

Trudy G started sputtering again but the whine of the mixer drowned her out. The thick white blocks of cheese were ripped apart by the beater blades, pulverized into a shapeless mass. Ha! Take that!

"You know," I hollered over the motor, "Baking can be quite physical. All that pounding and whipping and beating." I smashed an egg against the side of the Pyrex bowl and watched flecks of shell swirl into the batter along with the slimy streams of egg. "Oops," I said. "Look at that. Doesn't it just suck when you bite into a piece of eggshell?"

She grinned and gave me two thumbs up. I added 3 more eggs just as carefully. The bonehead and his pasty-faced child-bride could use the calcium.

"Trudy G, want to pass me the sugar bowl?"

"This one?" she pointed. "The one your reject, doorknob ex bought you at the farmer's market last summer?"

I nodded and reached for it, but damn, the thing slipped

from my hand and bounced crazily across the tile floor. We watched the sparkling trail of sugar filter into the wide grout lines. I looked gravely at Trudy G. "Hmm, didn't break."

She shrugged. "Quality goods. Who knew?"

"Gee, whiz," I said, "That was all the sugar I had. I guess I'm going to have to sweep this up and use it. I'm almost positive that I've washed the floor since Callie-Cat had her last fur ball episode.' I turned to fetch the broom, and then clumsy, single, ringless me, I stepped all over the sugar as I swept it up. The tea sieve worked great to filter out the floor crud, the big stuff anyway.

I measured a teaspoon of Mexican vanilla into the batter. "I'd really like to lace it with hemlock but unfortunately I'm all out."

Trudy G leapt off the counter. "Let me run out and get you some rat poison. Or a little Anthrax maybe. Woman has to keep up with the times, y'know."

I shook my head. "The scorned woman is always the first suspect, and prison stripes would make my ass look fat."

"Good point, girl friend. And you've just gotten over hating your mother for passing those bodacious hips on to you." She patted her own scrawny arse. "So can we stick that damn thing in the oven and go watch our movie?"

"Almost. Just need to add the chocolate. What did you rent?' I got to work stripping the foil-wrapped bars and chopping them viciously. A good sharp knife is a woman's friend. Dull knives leave clues.

She tapped the plastic case that was sticking out of her quilted handbag. "Evil Dead II: Dead by Dawn. As per your suggestion."

"Excellent." I folded the chocolate chunks into the batter.

Trudy examined the lumpy mixture. "Even with all the uh, accidents, it still just looks like the Supreme Chocolate-Chunk Cheesecake you took to Mike and Jay's last month."

"Almost," I smirked. 'This is Chocolate Explosion." I popped the cake into the oven and let the oven door slam. "Done. Let's movie. Do you want wine?"

"Of course I do. I'll pour." She filled two brandy snifters.

"Any of that chocolate left?"

"Since when does chocolate go with a Chilean Rose'?"

"Since when does chocolate NOT go with anything? Hand it

over," she demanded.

I handed it over. Trudy G read the label and sputtered, spraying wine all down the front of her white dollar store t-shirt. It made an interesting pattern.

"Did you really?" she choked out.

I smiled serenely. "Uhuh."

"High-five, Sister-friend," she squealed, slapping my hand as she tossed the last bar of Chocolate Ex-Lax into the garbage can.

Guilty as Sin

Stephanie Sesic Greer

When they first married, she remembers the oranges were delicious, fresh-squeezed like the light from the sun on each morning of the earth's new innocence.

But sometimes the apple's firm crunch becomes more necessary, and entanglements with worms can be a graceful, twining dance. She has never regretted the feeling of dirt between her toes.

Going Out

Laura Halferty

So here you are again. It's 2:00 a.m. on a Friday night and you find yourself in the sleaziest dive in the city.

This is the kind of place where you can't get a gin and tonic because there *is* no tonic. This is the kind of place where you can't get a beer in a bottle because bottles, in the wrong hands, become weapons. This is the kind of place where you wouldn't have been caught dead in your twenties because you'd never find THE MAN OF YOUR DREAMS here. But you've mellowed since then, and slumming it has a certain appeal.

Of course you haven't been here all night. This is just the place where you and Liz like to end up. You began the night's festivities at a classier joint—the kind of place where your shoes *don't* stick to the muck on the floor—and worked your way down.

The classy joint is a good place to build up a comfortable buzz on some other sucker's money and to dissect the week's events. You like to listen to Liz talk about her escapades. She's ballsier than you, and you both know it.

At the classy joint, you find yourself sitting next to an English professor whose condescending attitude lessens only slightly when he discovers that you've been educated in his discipline. He had wanted to believe you were just a pretty girl, but now he realizes that you're a body with a *mind* attached, and he's not sure he likes it. But then when he finds out that you never got your PhD, he settles back into smug superiority and magnanimously offers to buy you a drink. He whines about his slacking students, and you empathize with them because if he's *this* scintillating after work and semi-drunk, you can only imagine what goes on behind the doors of his classroom.

But you can only listen to him drone on about "deconstruction, post colonialism, blah blah blah" for so long. (Liz has conveniently escaped this torture by flirting with the cute bartender.) Even the promise of more free drinks can't keep you here. It's time to go somewhere livelier.

At the next place the doorman insists on seeing your ID, and this seems like a good omen.

You step into the crowd. There are beautiful boys everywhere, but the girls are catty and critical, and you watch *them* watch *you*. No detail of your going out get-up has gone unassessed. But you're above all this now. Turning thirty has liberated you from the company of this band of harpies.

The vibe is good for a while, but when the music becomes too ghetto for your tastes (you came of age in a decade when you'd never hear the word "nigger" in a club song, but were likely to be commanded to "Relax" or do "The Safety Dance"), you retreat to the perimeter.

After a few drinks, a glance at the clock tells you that it's time to head to the bar where you always end your night, the only place where you can shed your Pythian skin.

When you walk in, the atmosphere is comfortably hellish. The air is thick with smoke, bass thumping as you walk past the leering grotesques at the bar.

The first priority is drinks. You don't like beer in a can, they never have the ingredients for complicated drinks, and you hate the old stand-bys like rum and coke or a screwdriver. This leaves only one option: shots. You like the bracing, medicinal ones; Liz likes the sweet ones with seductive names. You order and survey the dance floor.

After a few shots you're loose enough to dance, and Liz knows you so well that you don't even have to say it. It's just a look and a nod and you're out on the floor.

And so you dance. Nothing matters but the dancing, and you don't stop until you hear the sound for last call.

Then the harsh lights are turned on you, like some nocturnal creature cornered. You don't want this night to end—not yet. You feel, always, that there is something left undone.

At home you'll collapse into bed, but too much stimulation and the smell of your stinking self (sweat, liquor, and smoke clinging to your hair) will conspire to keep you awake. So you'll

Women Behaving Badly

get into the shower, where your mascara will bleed down your face and you'll wash away the night's happy filth.

Tomorrow you step back into your real life, waiting for you there at home like the dog you don't have.

Dykes to Watch Out For

Mark Foss

On Tuesday afternoon, the day after Lisa and Murray move in together, Brie shows up uninvited with new hair.

"Wild strawberry," she announces.

"Tasty," says Lisa, patting the bristles on Brie's cropped head.

Up till now, Murray has longed for Brie to stick with one flavor and one girlfriend and give them some peace. But it's okay now: Murray has finally vanquished Brie—Lisa's oldest friend, self-appointed chaperone and defender of all things lesbian. He decides to take the high road, to be magnanimous in victory.

While he and Lisa go back to unwrapping pots and pans, Brie sticks her housewarming gift on the refrigerator door: a "Dykes To Watch Out For" comic strip.

"It's not going to bother the boss, is it?" says Brie, jerking her thumb in Murray's direction.

"He's broken in," says Lisa.

"Already? Too bad," says Brie. "I was hoping for a fight."

"With you? The human ice cream cone?" Murray says.

"You wanna lick?"

She pushes her head up against him, and she's so much shorter that her bristles fit under his chin.

"Oh, Murray, you make me melt!" She leans back, blowing him a kiss, swooning into Lisa's arms for his benefit. Lisa, who is only a few inches shorter than he is, captures her easily. They've done this routine before and he gives them his best bored look to prove it.

"The pots?" he says, finally.

"Relax," says Lisa. "We're half way through the kitchen boxes." She picks up her master list from the kitchen counter and waves it. "Only six more to go."

"Where's the vibrator?" Brie says, looking at the list in

pseudo-innocence. "You know, the one I got for you? I could warm it up."

"I replaced it," he says, lying. "And the new one is recharging. Thanks anyway." He refuses to let Brie get under his skin, but once again, he wonders if she and Lisa have simply talked about sex, or whether it's gone further than that.

Brie moves into the living room, and pulls out Lisa's Marlene Dietrich poster from a stack of prints leaning against the wall.

"Hmmm," she says, eyeing the walls.

"We can work it out without you," he says.

"I doubt that," she answers. She roots through another pile and finds "The Broadsword and the Beast," a promotional poster for a Jethro Tull album. He hasn't had it up in years, but it's a reminder of his past that he can't quite part with.

"Jethro Tull, Murray?" Brie says. "Lisa and I listened to that guy when we were twelve. Look at this sword. It's so phallic." She leans the poster with its face against the wall and then backs away slowly, as if the beast was about to leap off the paper.

"Please don't tell anyone I even saw this," she says.

"Don't worry," says Lisa. "Jethro's going in the trash this week."

He wants to say that Tull is a them, not a him, but it's already too late for a come-back. Brie prances around on one leg, playing air flute and Lisa pretends to play power chords on guitar. He didn't want the poster up anyway, but they don't leave much room for an honorable exit.

On Saturday night, Lisa is picking up treats for dessert when Brie arrives for dinner. Her hair is still strawberry. She plunks a bottle of wine down on the counter and eyes the home improvements they've made during their first week.

"Not bad," she says. "I see the Lisa touch."

She peers into the oven.

"Lisa always loved Home-Ec. It must have been that Easy-Bake oven I got for her seventh birthday."

"I suppose you never had girl toys."

"Oh sure I did. Lisa had a Barbie doll and I had Midge, Barbie's friend. But you know what, Murray? We never had a Ken.

We didn't need him. Although I'm sure Ken wished he could have been there, if only to watch what we did."

She takes a beer out of the refrigerator and moves to the futon in the living room. He stands against the window on the other side of the room. With Brie sitting down, he towers over her. All right, he thinks, you want a fight? You've got one.

"Take a load off, Murray."

"No thanks. I like it up here."

Brie smirks, and he smirks back. Neither of them will let down their defenses long enough to have a real conversation.

"You know Brie," he says, "I doubt Ken would have been that interested in watching Barbie and Midge. He was probably just waiting for Midge to piss off."

"He would have waited a long time."

"Maybe Barbie would have told her to get lost."

"I doubt that. They were best friends, you know. They did everything together. They even made love a few times, when they were young. But then Barbie started messing around with boys."

"Barbie came to her senses."

"No, Murray, I don't think so. She was always a conformist, our Barbie. It was just easier for her to be with boys. But Midge always knew that sooner or later, Barbie would come home."

A few moments later, they hear Lisa at the front door.

"She's home," Brie says.

"Hey you," Lisa says, looking at him. "You're supposed to be making a salad."

"That's telling him," Brie says. "You had me worried. I thought you were becoming 'The Happy Homemaker.'"

"Brie!" she says, as Murray heads for the bathroom to wash up. "Just because I've moved in with a man, you think I've lost it?"

As he moves farther down the hall, he can tell their voices have dropped. He hears whispers and giggles. He doesn't use the toilet, but he flushes it anyway and brings the seat up. Then he spots the Jethro Tull poster in the den. He tucks it under one arm and picks up the hammer and a couple of nails.

Oh, To Lie in Your Arms

Jenny Yasi

He was an ugly man, but his New York accent turned me on completely. Sheer exhaustion made me imagine how it would feel to have him holding me, one hand on my belly, another stroking my head. I was such a long way from home, and it was so cold.

"My parents make pianos," he said. "The business has been in the family four generations."

I trifled with the baby grand. "Do you play?" I asked him. The conversation bored me. I was pissed off at someone. Everyone.

"Not really," he said. "I can doodle. My girlfriend is great at it, though." His whole body was stiff. I played with my zipper vest, scalp crawling from miles bicycled across bridges and under-passes and ramps through the ugliest sprawl of New York.

"Pardon me, I think I stink," I said. We laughed. Ha, ha. I was toxically filthy with exhaust and bike grease.

"Saint James is an interesting name. Is it French?" he asked me, "or English?"

Honey save me, I was suddenly disgusted with that sticky sur-name, stuck like tissue paper to my shoe. And to think, I had ex-pected New York would save me from it.

"Hungarian."

"Oh." I think this confused him. So he asked, "And you're divorced?"

At that moment, coincidentally congested, I snorted into the kitchen, while he looked for a tissue. The air was like Nana's in Lynn, chlorinated water boiling into tea. Everything I owned was in panniers leaning against the door—notebooks, clothes, six hundred dollars in traveler's checks. I was too tired to think about divorce. "Can I use your phone?" I asked, thinking I could call home from there.

But he replied rudely: "I mean, your sister said you were married."

Now this guy's accent really annoyed me. I asked for aspirin. The back of my eyes swelled, trapped between the chlorinated air and old dried up bourgeois blood. I felt motion sickness.

"Never mind." He sensed the conversation was going wrong. He said, "Are you feeling … okay? You look distraught."

My face let go at the neck.

"He's dead." I wailed, and it surprised us both. My tears began dumping out onto my hands and sleeves, which pushed them back up as though they could be wedged back in my eyes.

"I'm sorry?" he asked.

"Well," and I found I could imagine this perfectly, "We were walking along the side of the road … "

"Yes?"

"A busy road near my house," I continued cautiously, and his weedy brown eyes finally met mine directly, glistening almost warmly. Soft white palms opened compassionately toward me.

"We were holding hands." He smiled as I spoke, so I took a deep breath. No need to rush. "The impact practically tore my arm out of my shoulder. Killed him instantly." And quite naturally, I sobbed, uncontrollably, shedding disgusting gobs of mucous, dust and accumulated toxins. "My arm still bothers me sometimes."

"I didn't know." So New York. How would he? His tweed-covered arm shyly floated up to comfort my sorry shoulders.

"Thank God he had sensed the car coming towards, and pushed us closer to the edge," I went on, imagining my future ex-husband as my hero, "or I would be dead too."

The piano heir's other arm, lost without its mate, also buoyed up in terror, clawing me into an awkward embrace. We stopped at the foot of mahogany stairs, panting like the traffic, just long enough for me to warm his scratchy neck, to make him sigh and lean closer.

As Is

Ellen Parker

Phone rings in Jane's cubicle.

She picks it up. It's Jerry, the Copy Center Guy.

"Jerry, it's not finished. I know, I know. What time is it? Oh, shit."

She hangs up. Yells down the row of cubicles, "Maggie! Three hours!" Goes back to proofreading Section 5, System Configuration.

Because it was completely rewritten and resubmitted by the proposal manager, Gilbert the Goddamn Fucking Spookiest Gearhead in the Goddamn Fucking Entire Solar System, a mere three hours ago (back at 1:42 a.m.) it is 279 pages of unedited gobbledygook, which is to say it comprises nothing but:

* misspelled words
* undefined acronyms
* impossible formulas
* ungrammatical sentences
* absent punctuation
* blathering gibberish

I can't fix this.

Jane lowers her face to the page and rests her cheek there. Her mind takes her outside, where she imagines she hears, from the depths of Puget Sound, the baleful cry of an Orca.

Jane, the lead editor of this proposal to design and build a 29-million-dollar Low-Frequency Active Transit Subsystem (LFATS) for the U.S. Navy's Poseidon-class submarines, at this moment, has a revelation.

Which is:

Unless she and Jerry the Copy Center Guy begin Xeroxing and collating and binding the required ten copies of the 1,100-

plus-page proposal, which amounts to 11,100-plus total pieces of paper all assembled in the proper page-number order, right now, there is no fucking way they will make the 8 a.m. deadline.

The proposal has to go out as is.

She rushes into Word Processing. "Stop!" Jane howls.

The bluish faces of Maggie and Ernie and Joelle and the seven unfamiliar temps stare at her, gaping, from behind their computer screens.

She runs from workstation to workstation, amassing pages.

"But … !" says one of the temps, an owlish girl with oily, lank hair.

Cradling the discombobulated paper stack, Jane rushes to her cubicle.

On the phone: "Jerry! I have it!"

And she scoops up Section 5 and shoves it between 4 and 6 as she runs.

The hallway is dark. At the elevator, she high-kicks the Down button. She enters, descends to the Copy Center.

Doors retract; she's out. She looks to her left. The cafeteria doors stand open. The doors to the deck stand open.

Hey. Air.

She wends her way through the maze of tables and exits to the outside world.

Ah, the view. She gasps. The black waters of Puget Sound. The brave little lights of the crossing ferry. The silhouettes of fir trees on the far shore.

The wind. Blowing fast to the waves.

She opens her arms.

Hurrah!

And she watches the pages billow and float and soar like a flock of pale nighthawks heading nestward, beating the dawn, weary.

Turn of the Century Woman

Katherine Ludwig

I'm just an old woman. I'm as poor and as ugly as anybody, but I never carried on the way them upstairs do. They think they got it worse than the rest of us. They don't. They don't beg for pennies all day like I do. They don't see those fancy people who look down on me like I ain't even human. They don't live most of each day alone.

Those people who throw me a penny and a look of pity or fear think I got no heart and soul. Well, good for them. I end up with a handful of coins for my trouble and when Teddy gets back with my pail, I'll have a cool drink of the fizzy stuff for my day's work. I like to feel it, cool and foamy, in my mouth, and then in my throat, and then going down my pipes before it swirls and sloshes around in my gut. My first taste is always a big gulp, the rest are small sips, to make the liquid last.

Teddy lives upstairs. I don't think they have nuthin pretty up there. He likes to look at the little framed painting I have. He looks and looks, his mouth hanging open, his eyes kinda glazed, like he never saw nuthin nice before. I'm sorry for him and his sister, with all the screaming and furniture breaking that goes on up there. Ya never hear any singing like from every other flat. Never any laughing. Never nuthin but that miserable drunk of a father and even worse mother, beating on each other and their kids. So Teddy—he must be nine years old—fights with the neighbor boys, getting all bloody and bruised most every day, but how is he supposed to know any better? Does anybody teach him anything else? And that poor girl, that poor, pretty girl. She tries to take care of her little brother but he's got no appreciation; pushing her away and even calling her names no young girl should ever even hear. She tries to clean the rooms they live in, and take care of that baby, but it ain't never good enough. I hear what goes on up there. I hear the hitting and the screaming and the crying. There's no way not to.

And Teddy, he runs away, he don't protect his sister. I guess I don't blame him. Anyway, I kinda like it when he runs down the flight of stairs and I open my door quick enough so he stops to pay me a visit. I like it. But the girl is stuck in there, like a flower growing outa the filth that's been swept into the corner of a dirty, stinking flat.

I know I'm gnarled and wrinkled and look a little hideous even, but I ain't a hideous person; I got a painting of a church, and I like to look at it.

Now where is that Teddy with my pail of stout? I'm gonna share it, so he keeps on coming to see me.

Step Away from the Knife

Kathrine L. Wright

"Never" was a girl without regrets. By girl, I mean loosely so. By regrets, I mean, well, you pick. Never flew airplanes out of hangars because she could. (Easier than you think in South Florida: Can't vote, can't drive, can't keep tabs on their oh so too much.) When stars shot skewampus from the sky, you can be sure Never had something to do with it. When traffic signs disappeared, you guessed it. It was Never.

Never was named by mistake, a typo, one simple keystroke that took her from Nevel to Never. You can imagine it all goes downhill from there. Never skipped jury duty, forgot parking tickets, left the dates that looked like the short man from Children of the Corn, right there in the middle of the restaurant. Later she would call her friends: Why him? she would say. Why?

Never borrowed cars from the snowbirds next to her, and next to her on the other side, and next to her across the street. She'd use them to carry groceries to the migrant farm workers who lived in the rusted trailers not one mile from her pious little gated community. Chicken and fruit leather and boxes and boxes of baked goods: Flatbread and whole grain and rye. The community patrol, the snowbirds? Never knew how the cars ended up in the wrong driveways.

Never couldn't love the boys who loved her. They loved the bad in her, which of course sucked the air right clean from her trachea.

When she dreamed, whole galaxies collapsed in on themselves. Her name was never Never. Waverly, it was. When she dreamed, colors shot by in parallel, and she moved so swiftly she was sure Waverly would explode. Snappy turtles surfaced and lulled her awake with Vonnegut and Muir and alligators brought her trinkets from their wondrous, winding canals.

Never thinks we're all just one slice away from dismantling. You and me, not her. Never spins clay around, around, around on a wheel until it makes something beautiful she never (always) intended.

Aunt Ruth's Karma

Cynthia Price Reedy

I bent over, shook my finger in Phydeau's face and said, "Bad dog. Bad, bad dog. Shame on you for lifting your leg on the couch."

Phydeau is fairly new to our household. Phydeau is fairly new, period. I've been cleaning up after him and throwing him out into the yard for four months now and am beginning to despair of his trainability. I am also beginning to wonder how long "cute" will keep me from throttling the little bugger.

His latest failing was overshadowed by the ringing of the front doorbell. There stood my husband's Aunt Ruth. She is the sourest person I've ever known. She rarely darkens our door, thank heaven.

"Where is my wretched nephew?" she demanded, sweeping past me into the interior.

I took a deep breath and consulted my watch. "It's three o'clock, so I rather imagine he's still at work."

"Well, tell him to come home at once."

Another deep breath. "Is there a problem, Ruth? Perhaps I can help, as it would be difficult for Philip to leave work early."

"Difficult? I am sure that is no concern of mine. Call him at once, if you please, young woman."

I gritted my teeth. I had promised Philip I would not fight with his aunt, as it causes repercussions through the whole family. So I said nary a word—even when Phydeau sniffed the back of Aunt Ruth's shoe and lifted his leg.

Ruth gasped and stood up ramrod straight. Her lips opened and closed like a beached fish but nothing came out. Her face went from red to purple.

Oh, God, I thought, she's going to have a stroke right here in the front hall. I reached for her to get her to a chair and the old bird brought up her fist and smacked me a hard one in the kisser.

It was my turn to gasp, which I did, and go rigid, which I did, and turn from red to purple.

I smacked Aunt Ruth back, hard enough to make her nose bleed. We stood in absolute silence, eyeing each other, as the ticking clock echoed in the room. Phydeau, wisely, said nothing.

Aunt Ruth threw her head back and opened her mouth and I was sure her heart was quitting and I would rot in prison for killing her, accidental or not.

Deep, honking noises huffed out of her mouth. Her shoulders shook. My mouth dropped as I realized the noises were belly laughs, great noisy guffaws.

Philip arrived home at 5:30, kissed me and said, "What shall we do for dinner, honey?"

I smiled. "I'm afraid you'll have to rustle something up on your own. I have to be at the YMCA at 6:30. Aunt Ruth and I have signed up for yoga."

Seating Arrangements

Nina Gaby

Dedicated to all the women who, for millennia, had to sit somewhere else

It was one of those things that had made her want to move to Vermont in the first place. Not just the practice of the Annual Town Meeting, actually, but all those little quirks, the peccadilloes of small town life. And of course there were the clear starry nights reflecting off the pure white crust of snow, the whole Norman Rockwellness and everything else that made her new town so special. Special enough to pull up all the safe stakes, throw the whole deck into the air and play Fifty-Two Pick-Up with the fallout.

"I worked my way up to VP of Corporate Marketing, for God's sake," she argued with her mother early on in the moving process. "I really can do anything if I can do that."

Her mother "yes-butted" for a few futile moments, but there was no dealing with Kate when the wanderlust hit. The once tow-headed toddler who had clung so desperately to her legs at nursery school drop-off time had grown first into a fearless and terrifying adolescent and now was an unstoppable force. "But rural New England, Kate? It's so different there. Have you done your research? Or did you just fall in love?"

"Of course I have. Done my research." Kate knew full well that she was moving to a state where it was easier to marry your first cousin than to put up a fence when you were sick of watching the rust sliding off of your neighbor's trailer. "And no, I didn't just fall in love. This move is a well-thought out plan. And Mom, you could do a lot worse than having family to visit in such a beautiful place." Rusty trailers notwithstanding.

Caught up in her enthusiasm on the morning of her first town meeting, she had failed to notice the seating arrangements when she arrived in the elementary school's all-purpose room. In fact, she had missed the room's dynamic altogether. Not unlike an all-purpose room in any school, the place smelled of old spaghetti, plasticene, vomit, and new books. . "I really think that the familiar smell led to my behavior," she admitted, later, to her mom on the phone.

Paying no attention to aforesaid dynamic, she had plopped down near the front row, proudly brandishing her sticky-back name tag and her "I voted today" button. Kate sat by herself. She hadn't yet met most of the folks seated around her on the old scratched metal folding chairs. She did notice the people seated facing the audience at two long folding tables were all men. Smiling men. Smiling at each other and at the man seated, not at the table with them, but facing them, just off to the left, in the row in front of her.

"He was like a shill, Mom," she described this to her mother later. The center of her cheeks still hot in two distinct spots. "Well you can't know everything, darling." Her mother was always supportive. It was like the time in Junior High when she took on the seventh-grade French teacher (and the whole Language Department) for using the phrase "Jewing down."

Meeting day was a huge flour sifter. A cloudy event full of intrigue and politics and the clear settling out of layer upon layer. The men in the front smiled often at one another. The man on the side rallied as if on invisible cue whenever needed. The issues may have been trivial by global standards: the expense of operating the two street lights; by-laws concerning the erection of cell towers; an obscure zoning issue that no one seemed to want to talk about.

People standing along the perimeter of the room, hanging around the back were dressed differently than those seated. Those at the back were dressed not unlike Kate in their Eddie Bauer distressed leather jackets and boots with heels. It was a carefully framed collage of color and sound. Things were firsted and seconded too quickly for a newcomer, one without a sense of history or place or time, to grab onto.

Yet, it was not unlike Kate to speak up. Even had she been mentored in the ways of rural New England, it may have made absolutely no difference. In her vision of the world, a town meeting was just that; a forum, if you will, for the town. She paid her taxes. It was her town. It was her meeting.

Kate raised her hand as she saw others do. She waited. Then she stood up and introduced herself. The room went silent for a moment as Kate politely asked for some clarification on a situation which had flown through discussion to passage in what seemed a nanosecond.

"I don't know if he actually said 'little lady,' Mom. But it felt like it." Her mother made sympathetic murmuring sounds. A good mother does not add insult to injury. "Without clarification, the noise resumed and no one else at the town meeting seemed to notice that a huge injustice had been done. Not even the folks in the back with the good haircuts."

"The injustice being," she continued on, "is that at least one person in this town doesn't know what the fuck anyone is talking about!"

"Well I guess you will just have to run for public office and straighten them out," her mother said. It wasn't the first time her mother had made this suggestion. "Well, I guess."

She gazed out through her windows. Lifting a pane, she scooped some early spring snow from the sill and held it to her cheek. The stars winked at her as they settled over the rounded shadowy hills in the distance, like a bowl of diamonds being turned upside down.

Aboyer—The Little Announcer

Dorette Snover

Sitting at the café, on a soft spring morning in Paris, my first thoughts rest with my daughter, Cocotte. She'll be twelve in a few weeks. And I know I will see her before that. Maybe soon.

Maybe even today. "It's the ides of March," the lady in the pheasant hat, the coat of foxes, tells Guilard, my regular waiter.

On the streets, the mist is thick, as it always is before seven o'clock.

I pull back on the iron chair; it scrapes against the pavement and I face Montmarte and the graves. Every morning for the last six weeks, this same iron table at Cafe Brulot has waited for me. But there is plenty of room for Cocotte at my table. She would like ... will like ... the tall vase, fluted lips, the water rising half-way up the stem of the yellow rose, even the bubbles along the stem, especially the bubbles of air, and me, waiting, waiting for her.

I'm so sorry, Cocotte. So very sorry.

"The usual," I nod to Guilard, and he returns with two silver plates of glistening oysters, setting one in front of me and the other across the table. At her place. I squeeze the lemon over Cocotte's curling oysters, and then my own. I notice, for the first time, that the café's chairs are forged in the same manner as the iron fence surrounding the graves.

The fork's tines barely touch the ice, but the cold traveling up the handle almost burns my fingers. I cradle a rough oyster shell in my palm. The cool flesh of the sea slides down my throat.

Cocotte, I didn't know. I couldn't. Listen to me.

My face warms to the young sun as it circles the white blooming apple trees, giving me hope that I too could be released from the rages of winter. The delicate new leaves are the bright bright green of youth unfurling.

Dear Cocotte. I know she will still come. Come back. I've whispered to her in my dreams.

At Notre Dame the bells begin; chiming seven

The morning-people move about, crossing paths with those still occupied with the night.

And it is as if each is oblivious to the other's existence, ignorant of each other's importance in the plan. For the hour when the two cross, the night-people ending their time, and the day-persons just beginning, that hour holds the danger. Even the slight woman in the pheasant-plumed hat, cutting her croissant in bits to feed her small curly dog: she remains asleep too it seems, unaware whether she is a person of the day or of the night.

I sigh and wave my hand at Guilard. He removes the plate of empty shells and my glass, empty of Sancerre. He reaches for Cocotte's oyster plate, but I pull it away from him. When he returns, he slides a white cup topped with froth before me, and at Cocotte's place, a blue plate with a sugar-dusted croissant amande. Butter and almonds to tempt her to come out from hiding!

I pull a folded paper from my gold beaded bag, feeling the hard triangle inside. I fold back the paper, to reveal the tiny, the smallest imaginable, crumbling wedge of panforte. All that I have left of Cocotte. I raise it to my lips and kiss the memory of the rich scent: the bitter almonds, butter and black spices.

Oh, Cocotte. Can you forgive me? For I've listened, and listened for your voice. I listened at every stretch. At every turn of the road as I ran away from you.

And so I will wait here at the cafe. For us. I will watch you open your eyes again. I will watch you swallow art, tasting the colors of the city: apricots and pears. Your mouth will open, pink as rosebuds again, and breathe around the buttery tastes.

Yes, Paris! I understand why we must meet in the city of light. No other collections of hard butter blocks laid out as bridges, small birds of bitter almonds resting on branches above us in the cemetery, singing our songs, songs of the dead, honey flowing against the black spices and into light, could be more, more than what I've wanted, to bring us both back to life, than Paris.

Come back to me. *SShhhh*..Listen.

The Exit Meeting

Laura White Schuett

"I trust you," Lou had said when they made plans for her to pick him up. So, on discharge day, Peggie drove the new car, a zippy little Tracer that Lou bought for his own birthday present. Just as he directed, she parked it in the rear lot at Kingston Hospital in a spot without cars on either side. Still, she worried as she walked to the entrance, bone grinding bone under the weight of ragged purple clouds and the promise of rain. It was early, and the parking spaces were already filling up.

In their nineteen-year marriage, there'd been many exit meetings. Usually she didn't look forward to bringing him home, but this time he'd been nice. He said to the other patients, "This is my beautiful wife," and pulled the chair out for her more than once.

Three years back, Lou'd been sober for nine months, the time it takes to make a baby. Peggie thought about this a lot, even as she walked to the hospital entrance that day. She was thirty-eight when he carried a magazine ad for a red-hot 300 ZX in his breast pocket, presenting it at all of the AA meetings with a "ha, ha," and, "This is my higher power. This is all I need."

Peggie used to laugh, but sometimes she explained to the other members, shoulders drawn up, "He doesn't believe in God."

"Thank you for speaking for me," Lou had snapped.

Before, when he was in rehab at Hart Hospital-a dirty and much grayer place-his higher power was a photograph of his first wife, perpetually nineteen and full of white teeth. Even though they were married only ten months and she died a decade later, he kept the grief as his own.

Peggie preferred the 300 ZX.

This time was different. He cut the tips off three of his fingers and told his bosses at Jensen & Johnson Vitamins that he did it on purpose. They didn't know he drank and that his Midnight Blue Mercury Tracer was his higher power. "The bosses like me," he said to Peggie during one of their visits. "They don't send everybody a card and flowers. They don't promote a person twice in less than a year."

One of Lou's bosses, Murry Niblock, a man she'd never met, told Peggie on the phone that the hospital had a reputation for being successful. Other employees were as good as new after a stay there. She didn't know what to say. It was true that the rooms and halls were lighter and more colorful than the other places, but sometimes Peggie shrank away from the brightness and clatter.

Lou made things-a coaster, a coil pot, and a beaded necklace. That was different, too. And he wrote a lot about everything, except there wasn't much about Peggie. She saw it as a good sign. He wrote about his father drowning his puppy and never saying he loved him, about his mother losing her hair when she was thirty, and even about Alice, his first wife, and how he barely knew her. During Peggie's visits, he gave her his journal to read as they drank burnt coffee with sugar and creamer in the too noisy Activity Room. "I want you to know," he said with a winning intensity.

"How's the car?" Lou asked when Peggie finally reached the doctor's office, arthritis drilling into her pelvis and her brown curls damp and flat against her thin neck.

"It was a long walk."

"You parked it where I told you to?"

"Of course," she said.

At the Exit Meeting, the doctor, a spare-haired man with a flickering gaze, discussed Lou's outpatient treatment. She nodded, but she didn't listen, not really. There'd been a lot of discharge days.

And she would have kept her mouth shut, squeezed tight in a smile, if Lou hadn't said, "I've been celibate since my first wife. She was the love of my life."

Peggie looked from him to the doctor and then to the red blinking eye on the phone. "What?" she pushed out and sat straighter, small hands tight, white buds on her lap.

"I mean," he said, "until you."

The office was quiet except for the sigh of the chair cushion as the doctor shifted and flattened his palms together. Peggie knew Lou was afraid she'd say that he was a mean drunk, that he drove his first wife away with fists to her lips and threats to cook her on low, and that he didn't even know the poor woman had died until his mother sent him the obituary.

"We've been married nineteen years," she said to the red light, "I thought that counted for something."

After, as they lugged his bags to the Tracer, Lou said, "Why do you have to make me look bad?"

She trailed behind, shoes scraping the asphalt and the bellies of clouds dragging across the broken horizon. "Do you want me to drive?" she asked.

"It's my car. Just like it's my house, my paycheck, and my burden."

His palms thumped and fingers, three thick with white gauze, twitched against the steering wheel as he edged onto Southern Avenue, a narrow, quiet street.

Then it happened.

A van door winged out from the curb, and it folded like a lady's fan as Lou slammed on the brakes. It was too late. Glass shattered, and a sharp, grating groan came from the Tracer's bumper as Peggie struck the windshield once, twice, and then wobbled.

"Your head, your big head," Lou said. "I couldn't see." He jerked himself free of the shoulder belt and grabbed at the glove compartment. "Damn it. Damn it." He stumbled out of the Tracer. "Did you take anything from the car? Did you?"

Peggie squinted and peered at a splintered Lou through the tangle of cracks in the glass, the densest knot where her forehead hit.

A short man bundled with wrinkles dropped in front of the van door and said, "Oh shit. Oh shit." His lighted cigarette tapped at the air. "Is that your wife? She's bleeding."

Peggie pressed the sleeve of her blouse to her head as Lou searched the Tracer with his good hand.

"I'm moving it," he said, and drove to the nearest lot, parking as far out as he could and walking back on unsteady feet.

When the police officer asked Lou, "Where's your car, sir?" Lou pointed. Voice strained, the officer said, "There are over two hundred cars. Can you be more specific?"

Peggie said, "The Mercury Tracer." Lou winced. "I was trying to help."

"How do you help?" he hissed.

From his plaid recliner, Lou cried, "My car. My beautiful car. And you wanted it to happen. You always hated it." Peggie knew it was the thirty-second time he said this because she kept a tally on the pad of paper by the phone in the kitchen. It was the same tablet she used for grocery lists and messages from solicitors, names and numbers recorded out of courtesy and addressed, "Lou-."

"Come eat," she said, shuffling to the doorway, forehead tight and sore with stitches and bony knees throbbing.

"What for?"

She'd made pork chops without fat and scalloped potatoes without onions because that's the way he liked them, but she knew his drink anchored him for the night.

"I'm sorry my head got in the way," she said, hoping for some kind of peace, some kind of appeasement.

He humphed. And for the thirty-third time he said, "My car. You did it on purpose. It'll never be the same." Lou's eyes closed.

"I was trying to help. We can get it fixed."

"We? You mean me. It's always me."

Peggie marked another tally. Lou would be stuck on this until he had another glass or two. Before fear or dread could take hold, she turned back to the kitchen and reached for the vodka.

"Do you want another?"

"You'd like that, wouldn't you, Pigster?"

"No," she said, and then poured him a big, fat drink.

Princess

S. K. Rogers

Yes, you know her. A pop diva with a whole lot of attitude and curves, as well known for who she's dating as for what she sings. She's been trading up in the boyfriend department, from hairstylist to video director to boyband singer to actor pulling millions per role. Her ego has grown in proportion to each new acquisition.

She is my current employer.

My name is Nina West, and having graduated with an M.A. in music, I made an alarming discovery—I just wasn't good enough for the concert stage, and I absolutely hated teaching. So I've been sliding by playing various half-assed gigs for the past year—some studio work, some part time orchestra, and playing bass guitar for the occasional garage group. When the woman known familiarly in the music world as The Princess (though not to her face) decided that she needed some "street cred" in the form of a real backing band (as opposed to synthesizers), I was brought in by Zak, the guitar player, an old chum.

The Princess has an entire entourage, including a hairdresser, make-up person, stylist, personal trainer, yoga teacher, lifestyle coach, masseur, assorted personal assistants, and a poufy little dog who barks incessantly and has to be dosed periodically with canine Valium. The pooch's name is Queen's Fancy Royal Daughter, aka—you guessed it—Princess.

This has led to no end of hilarity among the crew, resulting as it does in such gems as "That god damned Princess peed on the dressing room floor," and considerable confusion, such as the time a new Personal Assistant mixed up the appointments for the human Princess's breast augmentation with the canine Princess's spay job. Whole new meaning to "getting fixed." And of course, when someone refers to "that bitch Princess" ...

So as we speak, the band is in Seattle for a charity bash, one of those things with twenty different groups playing for AIDS or whatever, and the Princess (human) is throwing a hissy fit because she's not getting enough attention. I'm in the cramped little dressing room the band shares (as opposed to the diva's luxurious quarters) when she comes stomping in.

She throws her long dark hair back in a patented tress-toss maneuver, flares her nostrils, and proclaims, "My flowers are the wrong color!"

"Bummer," I say. This is *so* not my department, but apparently for once there's no one else around for her to vent to.

"They're pink! Not peach, pink!"

"Yeah, well," I mutter.

"My rider specifies peach!"

I shrug. I wish I smoked; I could do that snotty inhale-and-blow thing, but since I have virgin lungs, I have to settle for a shrug. Behind her, the dog has started barking yet again.

"Do something about Princess!" commands the Princess as she flounces out. I think about pointing out that this is also *so* not my job, but what the hell; I don't want to listen to all that yapping either and at least I have the means to shut up the dog. I go into the main dressing room, and shake out a doggy downer from the pill bottle next to Princess's little travel kennel. I roll it in a Beefy Strip, and feed it to the princess pooch. She gulps it down eagerly, burps, and within the minute has subsided on her little silk pillow.

I contemplate the vial. Good stuff. I think about popping one myself. Or maybe five, I muse, that's a pretty small dog ...

Behind me, the Princess is saying imperiously, "Bring me some champagne!"

Right on cue, I think. I pick up the bottle of Cristalle from the bucket of ice.

Some say the least said about that show, the better.

But seriously, it was rather glorious.

Oh sure, her Highness was kind of out of it. Well, to be completely honest, she ended up slumping against an amp and slithering to the floor in the middle of the second number.

Zak, the guitar player, faltered, looked over at me. I kept playing, looked across at Dave the drummer, who shrugged, still banging away. The keyboard guy was just plugging along, in his own little world.

I looked out at the crowd, some 40,000 people. They deserved better than a half-baked egocentric pop Princess anyway. I took the tempo up to double time, segued into something new. Zak picked up, came in with a skanky chord. Shayla, the back up singer, realized what we were doing and stepped up to her mike.

And we totally rocked out an auditorium of prepubescent teenagers and their moms with a cover of The Clash's London Calling, a punk rock classic.

It was awesome.

Of course, we were all summarily fired that night. Packing my gear and wondering if I could talk one of the limo drivers into a ride to the bus station, I looked up to find Princess parked on top of a speaker cabinet, watching me glassily.

The dog, I mean.

"I'm gonna start a punk band," I say. She stares.

"Sorry about blowing your stash like that," I add.

And I could swear she winked at me, that Princess.

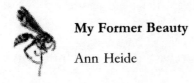

My Former Beauty

Ann Heide

Rosemary leans over me as I huddle beneath the downy duvet in the darkened bedroom. I've kept the lights off and the curtains closed since my accident. It doesn't seem long ago that Rosemary had *her* accident. She broke both her arms when she tumbled backwards all the way down the stairs of her house, her loaded dinner tray spiraling out of her hands and sailing over the banister to land foodless beside her at the bottom of the stairway. Rosemary crawled across the fragments of mashed potatoes and carrots to reach the phone in the hallway. She called 911.

"Did you black out?" the doctor asked her.

"No"

"Did you get dizzy?"

"No."

"Were you feeling ill?"

"No."

"What, then?"

"I just missed a step. That's all."

I spoke with Rosemary on the phone many times during the ordeal that followed but I never saw her in that broken state. I don't like visiting hospitals and besides, I'm unable to get out much socially these days. The streets are slippery in the winter and it's hot and muggy in the summer. As for spring and fall, they aren't real seasons in this part of the world. I'm always occupied, though. I have lots of appointments. There's my physiotherapist, for one, although I've not gone there much lately. He always wants me to do some sort of exercises, but I forget to do them or else I'm too busy. There's my hairdresser, of course, at least once a week; people have always told me I have beautiful hair. And I have to see doctors, lots of them. Gastroenterologist, podiatrist, gynaecologist, ophthalmologist, urologist. And now there will be dental and periodontal appointments too numerous to count.

"How are you, my dear?" Rosemary coos. "Poor you! You're a mess." Since she's already answered her own question, my immediate response is to burst into tears.

"My teeth! I've knocked out my front teeth! They were my two best ones," I gasp between racking sobs. "I need to get my strength up but how can I? I can't even eat."

"I had to be fed for three months when I was in the hospital" she replies. " I remember the sweet little nurses' aid who used to cut up the food and spoon it into my mouth. When I dribbled, she wiped my chin with a cloth." Rosemary looks at me solicitously.

"Don't look at me!" I command, holding a Kleenex over the lower half of my face.

Rosemary and I have been friends a long time. We've been around the block. Lots of water under the bridge. We're 'good buds', her teenaged granddaughter would say. The week that Rosemary fell at home and broke both her arms, another friend of mine fell in a restaurant and broke both her legs. When I told my son of these parallel misadventures, he burst into snorting laughter. I went into a fit of giggles myself, though it was far from funny. Well, I'm sure not laughing now.

"You'll be up and around in no time" says Rosemary "and dentists can do the most marvelous things today. Just wait, you'll be back to yourself in a few months."

"You don't understand. It's so horrible. I feel like killing myself!" Tears rolling down under the Kleenex onto my swollen lips.

"I was in rehab for six months," Rosemary recalls. "The doctors put nine metal pins in my right elbow. I thought I'd never be able to live normally again. But here I am!"

"But it's my front teeth, Rosemary!"

"They had to feed me, dress me, wash me. They even had to wipe my bum when I went to the bathroom and they had to pull up my underwear afterwards."

"I feel like taking all these pills!" I pick up a bottle of Tylenol 3 and slam it down on the night table. "Why did this have to happen to me? At my age?" Rosemary is almost ten years older than I am. You'd never guess her age; at eighty-four she stands straight, dresses ever so stylishly and there's that flaming red hair. Of course it's dyed, whose isn't? But it looks pretty good just the same. Rosemary's an attractive woman. Even her arms look strong and shapely to me, though I can't really see them under her sweater.

"Yes, it's awful. But you'll just have to be brave" she says firmly, setting her lips in a grim line. "Think of how much worse it could have been."

"Don't be mean to me!" I'm shouting now and the Kleenex has fallen away. "I need your sympathy. It's a terrible thing that's happened to me!" Rosemary sees my cracked lips with the stitches sticking out like cats' whiskers, the caked blood, and a cavernous abyss where my lovely teeth used to be.

"Don't worry," she admonishes, "You'll be restored to your former beauty. In fact, they'll give you perfect teeth, better than ever."

I pick up the photo from my bedside table. It was taken when I was in my mid twenties. Dark curly hair falling over my shoulders, flawless skin, sultry eyes, a broad smile displaying perfectly straight gleaming white teeth. "Just like this?" I ask.

"Just like that" she nods. I lay my weary head back on the pillow and Rosemary rises to leave. "By the way..." she asks, "how did you fall? What happened? Did you black out?"

"No"

"Did you get dizzy?"

"No."

"Were you feeling ill?"

"No."

"What, then?"

"I just missed a step. That's all."

A Perfect Family Dinner

William J. Bianchi, Jr.

Mary's stew simmered as she bent to check the hors d'oeuvres. Not quite crispy: they needed only another 12 minutes or so. Perfect. Bobby loved finger food best and Jim could never get enough meat and potatoes.

Her romance novel sat on the counter. Jim simply hated seeing them lying about so she covered it with a dishtowel. She looked the kitchen over once more and noticed the trash. "Oh, no!" Beer cans threatened to spill over the top and onto her clean floor.

Mary whisked the offending Hefty out the trailer's kitchen door and into the big rusted trashcan sitting by Jim's old Buick. The aluminum made that muffled rattle, and the familiar, warm stench of stale beer puffed in her face as she stuffed the bag down.

The telephone rang. "Hello." She nestled the phone between her shoulder and ear as she set the table with her grandmother's good china.

"Mary, are you all right?" Diane asked. "I just talked to Carl down at the hardware store and he said you had bruises all over your face. Which one of'em done it this time?"

"Come on, Diane, no need to get so melodramatic. I just tripped and fell."

"Sure. How many times is that in the past few months? Four?" Diane paused. "Damn them!"

"Calm down. Everything's fine, now." She set the silverware by her china plate, just so.

"I can't calm down and it's not fine. One of these days they're going to kill you."

"No one's going to kill anyone. Look, will you promise to be happy for me if I share some good news, something really wonderful?" Mary paused. "Last night we had a real heart-to-heart. I told Jim that things had to change."

"Leave their asses, Mary, both of them. That no-good, free-loading, thug son of yours ain't any better than Jim. They should have kept him in prison and never let him out for what he did to that poor Tucker girl."

Mary went on, "I laid out all the bad things that Jim's done and when I was through he felt so bad he got down on his knees and begged forgiveness. He even cried. On his knees with tears in his eyes, Diane! I wish you could have been there. It was the *most* romantic thing *ever*, even better than a Harlequin." She placed two candles in the center of the table.

"Pull your head out of those stupid books and wake up. You're living a horror, not a romance! What about Bob, huh? Did he cry too? He didn't, did he?"

"Well, no. But after my talk with Jim, Bobby said he was truly sorry and promised he'd start being the kind of son I always wanted. What more could a mother ask?"

"She could ask for, no, demand, a faithful husband who doesn't beat her, and a son who knows her name's not Bitch."

"Diane, please. It's not like that anymore. Things have finally changed for the better. Really. This is a new beginning for my family. I've even cooked a perfect dinner to celebrate."

"Honey, listen to me, OK? No matter what either of those dirt bags say, nothing's gonna change. Do you understand?"

"You're wrong. Look, I don't have time for this. I've got to get dinner on the table by six. Sharp. After twenty-six years of marriage, I deserve this one perfect family dinner with my adoring husband and loving son. I'll call you tomorrow."

"Wait, don't hang—"

Mary hung up. Diane just didn't understand. She didn't know how sweet and peaceful Jim could be after he had passed out on the couch. And Bobby. Diane didn't know how excited he got when she gave him money or the way he called her mommy when he asked. All Diane could see was the bad, the times they lost their tempers.

Enough of that. Tonight was about new beginnings and making her family right. Tonight, was about bringing her family together, at last, over a perfect dinner. The timer rang. Mary lit the candles and dimmed the lights. She almost called for Jim and Bobby, but thumped her palm against her forehead instead. "Good one, Mary. Jim's right. I'm as stupid as I am ugly."

Appetizer plate and spatula in hand, she opened the oven and scooped the hors d'oeuvres.

Crispy now, Bobby's fingers spilled onto her plate. She almost poured herself a bowl of Jim-stew but stopped. Perhaps revenge is best served cold and hard but just this once during dinner, she wanted her Jim warm and soft. She decided to wait and pour a bowl after the Bobby-fingers so it wouldn't cool.

At long last, the perfect family dinner.

All in Good Time

Ellen Parker

All her life, until she became Queen, she'd been waiting.

When she was a child, she'd waited to grow prettier than her stepmother. When she did, her life changed, as she'd known it would.

Shortly she found herself mothering seven little men who were hapless at anything else except mining priceless gems. She cooked for them, made their wee beds, wiped Sneezy's nose, and swept their floors with an inefficient broom that shed straw.

Alas, doing chores for seven small and very predictable people didn't fill her day. She found herself playing Solitaire a lot, and cheating. She found herself skipping around the parlor rug, using the shedding broom as her prince, and breaking into song. She found herself experimenting with different hairstyles, which upset the dwarves, so she stopped.

All of it was just a way to take her mind off the waiting.

No wonder she ate the apple. Its scrumptious redness lit up her life. That apple, which right then was more important to her mouth than a kiss could be, took her out of one phase of waiting and, after she died for a while and waited for rebirth, delivered her into another.

Now she was the Queen.

To help explain the frequent visits to the palace by seven short men, she retained all of them as Official Royal Advisers. She especially relied on advice from Grumpy, whose bad attitude helped her see another side of things.

"This is your life, girly," Grumpy told her. "Starting now."

"All I know how to do is keep house," she replied. "And wait."

"A Queen does neither. What does the King say?"

"He's never around."

"See! He's busy! What's he do all day?"

She shrugged. "I don_t know him well enough to ask."

He harrumphed. He threw the newspaper at her feet. "Find work."

She read the papers while pacing the floor. Shocked at the ugly state of affairs throughout her kingdom—breakouts of scabies, mule-cart gridlock, scatological troubadours, virgins eating poisoned apples—she slumped onto her throne.

And she set to work trying to right all the wrongs in her kingdom. Everywhere she was lauded for her beauty and her goodness.

I like this, she thought.

One day she learned she was pregnant. She kept working, wafting hither and thither in her designer muumuus, looking *mahvelous*. Soon enough she gave birth to a lovely baby girl.

Although she adored the little girl, she surely shouldn't spend her every waking moment doting over the pretty little princess, should she? She shouldn't toil in solitude with no one bearing witness except this wee pygmy that only drools? Didn't people hire nannies and maids and governesses for that sort of thing?

When the little princess came of age, the Queen proclaimed each day thereafter to be Take Your Royal Daughter to Work Day. When the canny little princess showed up, people fell all over themselves.

"How lovely she is!"

"How graceful!"

"How kind!"

"How effective!"

The Queen had an advisory session with Grumpy, while the little princess gamboled prettily past the doorway, happily playing hide-and-go-seek with the shape-shifting Royal Serpent.

"Lately I have begun to reevaluate—" the Queen began, tapping her teeth with her scepter.

The next thing she knew, Grumpy left the palace with the six other dwarves and the princess.

The Queen knew what was up.

Fine, she told herself. That spoiled little missy needs to do some housework.

Meantime, I'll plant the kingdom's most enticing apple tree.

"Red Delicious!" she cried aloud.

She knew the trees would take some time to bear fruit.
That's all well and good, she told herself.
I know how to wait.

On Sex

Vanessa Kulzer

I've had a lot of husbands. Or, I've been married many times. Not in the actual sense, but in the way that people are married through sex. It is a union of sorts, after all, I don't know how it is for everybody, but I like to memorize the person I'm having sex with. Which is usually a man, but you never know.

I like to smell their ears, hair, neck, armpits. I even smell their feet and their—as my Grandma would call it—"down-belows" I love the smells of a man. And I like to look at all the little parts of their bodies. I look at every hair follicle, pore, birthmark, mole.

I especially like a man's beard. It is so weird how they have all that bushy hair coming out of their faces. Imagine! I like to see where each little stalk of hair pokes out, and the patterns they make.

I had a boyfriend once that had every color of beard in his face, well, except grey because we were, like, young at the time. Three shades of brown, red, black, even a mutant clear one. Believe it or not, it was clear. Truly.

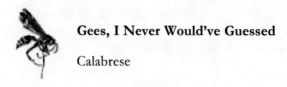

Gees, I Never Would've Guessed

Calabrese

Until I was eleven, I knew it all. Like I was gonna be the first CFL quarterback from Loggieville, New Brunswick. So what if I'm a girl? Then, three days before my eleventh birthday I got what Mom chirpily called my "little man".

I was not totally unprepared. I had the book Mom left—under my cereal bowl, in with my ironed underwear and finally inside my Tarzan comic. Mom was available for questions, if I had any, which she told me I wouldn't, so I didn't.

The book promised something magical was on its way to me. It had to do with my body and a threshold. It didn't mention blood. What stuck in my mind was this picture of an elastic contraption holding a gauze hammock. A hammock for what, wasn't clear. It got way too clear on that morning in '61 when I woke up with the flu. I planned to suffer it out on the field, anyway. The boys needed me. I was their dirtiest scrapper. But I was not ready to die for football and what else could this mess in my nightie mean!

"In the name of the nine blind snotty orphans, sit on that toilet and don't move!" I knew from these loving words that I was not about to die. "Better get used to it young lady. It's yours for the rest of your life."

And then there was that hammock again! Gees I never would'a guessed! My mother seemed really pleased with herself for rigging me up; just stood there smiling, waiting for me to feel, I don't know? Grateful? Fulfilled? I felt like a cowboy whose thighs would never meet, let alone touch again. I walked like I felt.

She added cornflakes—the kind you don't eat!—to our order from the general store. "Not for me either," Mom's voice dripped conspiracy. Somehow HER status had just gone up!

Confused I headed for the one thing I knew, football. I was

late for the game, but I took the time to slip behind the Fina station. That pad had been on me all of 15 minutes and twice I'd rescued it from my belly button. And once with a snap of elastic it got stuck between my shoulder blades. I threw the whole mess in the garbage.

The boys were cursing and fighting, waiting for me. We started right in. Third tackle left me a bloody mess.

"Jesus Mel, Ya didn't have to nail her that hard!"

One of the older boys started whispering and everyone was backing away.

The girls thought I had it made. A man, a home, babies just around the corner. I just soaked it up. They'd get theirs soon enough.

The boys mostly treated me like I was contagious. One guy did start hanging around. The girls thought I was crazy for ignoring dreamy Eldon. He'd spent two years in every grade so he had maturity and determination on his side. He looked alright. Too bad he had to open his stupid mouth. If he found me alone in the coatroom he'd whisper, "Old enough to bleed, old enough to butcher!" Too weird. Bad enough I got my period, and now I had to watch out for Eldon who for some reason wanted to slit my throat!

All this hassle and what for?

Then I kissed Keith at the top of the Ferris wheel. I thought I'd never come down. Once again, I knew it all. And it had nothing to do with football!

I started saving a seat on the bus, guarding the phone at home, wearing dresses to school, and praying for breasts.

Hard as I tried, I never did kiss Keith again. Every night I'd cram my head full of him, the bristles of his hair, his wide-set brown eyes. His nose was kinda cutesy for a guy so I'd change it a bit. Then I'd be at his lips and that kiss that tugged at my stomach and pressed my thighs together.

Most nights I did manage to dream of him. Sometimes it was Eldon. The kiss was the same. We'd kiss and kiss but no one knew where to go next. All that kissing and I'd wake up sweating every time, wondering what else my mother hadn't told me.

The Moon

Julie Hannah

I leaned against the bedroom door and watched my cousin Celeste. Perched on the stool in front of the dressing table, she gathered up curlers in one hand, arranged them in the other and made small talk. Her arrogance filled the room as she prattled on in the stultifying late afternoon humidity about yesterday's canasta game and the Women's Club

I tried to tune her out. I knew she wouldn't say what was really on her mind. She thought it should have been her Eleanor, not my Rachel, who got married earlier today. I'd returned to this empty house alone after the wedding. In the quiet, I pulled off my dress and damp under things and stood by the back window letting the breeze cool my skin.

When I heard Celeste's footsteps mincing across the hardwood in the front room, I'd barely had time to grab my dress and drop it over my head before she barged uninvited into the bedroom. I'd grown up in this house next door to my cousin. She'd snatched my toys when we were small, and when we were older, just as freely made off with the contents of my closet. "You'd be more popular if you'd try a little," she'd once said as we waited on the porch for yet another of my boyfriends to come pick her up. But her attempts to steal the handsome Tom for Eleanor hadn't worked; he'd had eyes only for Rachel. Now, loathing scalded my insides like hot coals at the memory of her treachery.

With hardly a second's forethought, I turned and lifted my dress to my waist, thrust out my bare behind, then quickly let the dress drop. A rain of curlers pelted my butt and peppered the floor around me.

Without looking back, I slammed the bedroom door behind me, strode across the living room and came face-to-face with Hector Sands at the front door. He'd been a year ahead of me in school. Now high school principal, he and Celeste co-chaired the planning committee for this years' Homecoming celebration. "Is Celeste here?" he asked. "I saw her car out front." "Yes," I said. "Come in." I picked up my purse and shoes from the floor by the sofa.

A devilish thought occurred to me. Celeste could never pass up a chance to repay an insult. I returned to the bedroom door, knocked, then shouted, "Oh, Celeste, dear." To Hector I said, "Just wait a second," and waved my hand at the cushioned arm-chair. I walked out of the house and continued across the front porch, leaving poor Hector sitting facing the bedroom. Halfway down the steps I heard Celeste's agonized shriek. Hector flew past me, his face crimson.

By the time I reached the car I shook with laughter. In the rearview mirror I saw Celeste on the porch, fists clinched, her face a mix of fury and embarrassment. With no destination in mind, I drove out of town past brown fields of milo. I wound up at the lake where my family had spent so many summer days. At the end of the wooden pier I sat and dangled my bare feet over the edge. While the sky turned rosy, then orchid, and finally pur-ple, I contemplated this improbable afternoon. In the deepening chill, that huge yellow orb emerged from behind light clouds and spangles danced on the dark water. I laughed out loud.

Marital Problems

Cynthia Price Reedy

Damn, thought Dick. She's a raving maniac and she's on the loose—again! Why can't those people at Shady Vale keep Jane nailed down?

He stepped to the back door and stood perusing the large panel inset next to it. He punched three buttons, sending electricity coursing through the perimeter fence. He's had bison fence installed and it carried a massive jolt—more than the law allowed, really. The next button pushed open the door to the kennel, letting three rottweilers the size of small ponies loose into the yard.

Hope they work, Dick thought. When Jane's on a tear she's meaner than all of them put together.

He decided against the sonar to detect tunneling—she hadn't been out that long. He *did* start the radar dish circling on the roof and pulled the plastic cover off the screen.

Those tasks done, Dick poured himself four fingers of scotch and stood at the window, idly shifting his glance between the horizon, the sky and the screen.

There was a rapid blip that appeared on the screen but it was moving so fast that seeing it was no help to him,

"My God," he said, as a Scud missile ripped through the roof.

CRAP, Co.

Katie Haegle

After I read Willy Wonka in the fifth grade, I informed my dad that Roald Dahl once worked in a chocolate factory, and that this was the inspiration for his book. He smirked and told me about his high school job hosing down machines at a diaper cleaning facility.

"Maybe I should write a book about that and call it Monty and the Shit Bag."

Like my dad, I eventually got my own crummy first job, as a writer for the Central Regional Associated Publishing Company. It wasn't lost on me that the place's acronym was CRAP, but I thought a real writing job would have made my dad proud. He'd been dead for two months by then. I still thought about him all the time.

CRAP Co. published trade magazines, which are niche publications for different industries. The magazine that hired me was called "Direct Marketing Professionals Monthly." Direct marketing professionals, incidentally, are the people whose trade is "lists," as in lists of your phone number and address. The people who call you during supper and sex. I had to interview these people and profile them; I had to give them tips on how to get access to unlisted numbers; I had to write zealous updates on anti-spam legislation. I did this for as long as I could each day, and then I crept into the conference room and cried.

Almost redundantly, my boss tortured me. Nessa was one of those supercharged petite women who was always, always the first person to arrive at the office. Each morning when I got in she squealed "Good MORNing!" as if to say: I will always be the one to greet you.

Early on I made a project of online job searching that eventually devolved into just searching for magazines that seemed even worse than my own. One day I found a fishing magazine called Crappie World. As I fantasized about working there as a receptionist ("Hello, you've reached Crappy World") Nessa charged in.

"Good AfterNOON! Denny is taking us to lunch today. Wear lipstick!"

Denny was our elusive editor-in-chief. He was too important to mix it up with us, but I knew about him from his superfluous Editor's Notes, which he packed with posh details of his life. He and his wife preferred WholeFoods' hand-rubbed Tibetan wheat with their Organic Peking. He and his wife had been on two photographic safaris in Africa that restored their belief in God, "such a majestic land it was." There was no disputing his role as the chief officer of CRAP.

We went out to the front of the building to wait for him, and when his car pulled up my stomach gave a nasty lurch. Since my dad died I'd done a few double takes, thinking I'd seen him, alive again, on the street or train or in line at the bank. On second glance it was always an old man, someone with bleached skin stretched over a bony skull. Dad had been so ill for so long that he didn't look his age when he died, and I'd almost forgotten he was ever young, ever not sick.

But here was Denny, a healthy and middle-aged doppelganger, resembling my dad down to his German-English-whatever blend of features, his thinning but still-there hair. Dread bloomed in my middle like an ugly black flower.

During lunch I was tacked like a bug under Denny's dad-like gaze, too stunned even to get up and use the ladies' room. Denny/Dad talked on and on, occasionally making me jump by laughing too loudly. I couldn't believe it. He had just the same swagger my dad got when he was feeling especially consumer capitalist, a feature I'd somehow erased from my memory. It was as if, for laughs, God had taken my father's worst traits and presented them to me all at once, like an ungentle prod: Get over it already! He wasn't always that great! Remember when he made you take the high school placement test even though you had a fever of 101?

I was dying to smoke; I kept swilling ice water instead. By dessert—Denny had the Albanian cheesecake with fresh passion-fruit drizzle—my distended bladder pressed painfully against the waistband of my skirt. When lunch finally ended I stood warily, teeteringly, like the Statue of Liberty being raised.

In the car I sat next to Denny/Dad, and I had to pee so bad tears stung my eyes. I pasted a smile on my face and left it there for the duration of the painful stop-and-start ride. In the foyer I shouted brightly, "I think I'll take the stairs, walk off some of that delicious lunch!" Nessa looked perplexed and walked toward the elevator. Denny, half-tanked on martinis, just shrugged.

I had only peed my pants once as a little kid, right outside my own house, because I hadn't gone all day at school and just couldn't make it one step further. Looking back, it was as if the reassuring sight of my house was enough to loosen my bladder, and the warm liquid gluing my jeans to my legs felt almost pleasant: proof of how safe I finally was. I guess that's sort of what happened that day. The moment I stepped into the dim stairwell I let loose, pee blossoming against my legs and turning my dark green pants darker. I scuffled up the stairs, pretending to myself I was still trying to make it to the bathroom, but in reality loving the sensation of letting go. I had a primal feeling of protecting myself from the world—a porcupine with her quills, a skunk with spray. I hobbled through the lobby to the bathroom, turned the hand dryer on my legs for 40 minutes, and returned to my desk, swaddled in my cardigan from the waist down.

"You did so well at lunch today," Nessa said too kindly. Her nose twitched. She never let on that she knew what happened that day, and she never was unkind to me again

And me? I stayed on CRAP Co. But there was no reason for me to hide anything, anymore. I simply acted impudent and lazy and rude and blamed my job for my unending misery.

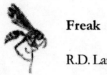

Freak

R.D. Larson

The minute I walked into the new schoolroom, I could feel it. Do you know? That sickening, hating, scary feeling? Black Italian eyes slid away, not meeting mine. Shoulders jutted in my direction. I heard words that I could not understand and mocking laughter I could.

Oh, sure, I tried to be nice, but they had known each other for years. They had backgrounds, foods, skin color in common. They pulled my white curly braids and called me "Albino!"

The boys farted at me.

Ha! So what? My noodle brother had taught me to fart good. So I did, and arm-wrestled, too, those tough little Italian boys. Even those smart-alecky girls decided this skinny Irish kid wasn't so bad by the end of the first week.

Occupation

Jason Nelson

I've seen hope. Not in the eyes of children, or in some wacky over-used metaphor, rather I have seen an actual, physical hope. It's not a place filled with broad clean streets and gas stations closed on Sundays. There aren't pictures of hope in glossy magazines circulated through national subscription services. Hope isn't a mineral or animal, a liquid or gaseous excretion. There's a woman, I can't tell you where, who makes hope. Her fingers don't bleed when she creates, like those who make inspiration. She reaches no transcendental state, like the man who manufactures tolerance and the occasional batch of hurried excitement. In fact, like all facts, she, this women who builds hope, finds her task boring and predictable. The exact process for making and the chemical composition of hope aren't exactly secrets, as much as they are just uninteresting lines of words and awkwardly connected syllables, easily forgotten. She dearly wanted to be a veterinarian, working with cats and dogs and cats again. But then dreams aren't meant for hope, she so often repeats while methodically assembling hope after hope after hope.

All Your Money

Lisa Selin Davis

Have you ever wanted to give someone all your money? --Norman Dubie

I.

The image is of faces pressed against windowpanes on a frosty night; breath, condensation painting ghosts of eyes, nose, mouth on the glass. Is that what you meant? That image stays a moment, maybe two, and then evaporates like invisible ink.

Once, maybe last week, at a bar, I was standing and you were sitting and you looked up at me. My feet lifted off the ground, just for a second. I thought I knew then what the other little girls did at slumber parties, incantations and two fingers stretched towards a lifeless body to make it rise. I thought, Now? But you blinked.

You said this never happened to you. You said, Can you feel me on this? You said, The crowd never parted for me, revealing a beautiful girl with a daffodil mouth in a red dress waiting patiently.

You said you were a fan of Bach (You think he cares? asked my husband. He's dead). And you explained—what enunciation, like you kissed every word—the foresight of Johann Sebastian, early rock and roller, the old 1-4-5 chord progression and a whole symphony to get there.

I forgot to stand. I asked the bartender, what's the deal with that woman? She's crazy, he said, and I moved to the other side, next to you, and bought you bourbon with my last three dollars. I pulled the cotton from my pockets to show you Just How Empty.

With your lover's credit card, you bought the almost good stuff—Knob Creek and Makers Mark—and we walked back towards your apartment.

It was far too cold. We passed a cornfield. You said, Let's go in, I said, No. But you were gone already, running in circles, your tail made of whisky and wind. You ripped the ears from their stalks and I yelled, It won't be any good. You said, It will.

You remind me of an old brown down with floppy ears, you said, floppy years, one small fleck of white on its chest like a crucifix. You appeared from the field with your bouquet of unripe maize, your white shirt stained. You insisted that we cook the stuff, green kernels. It's bad, I said. And you said, Yes.

I thought that would be the end, but you are still here, fading in and out like frost on the windowpane.

I have this idea—you know what it is, I tell you every day. It takes an army to calm the thing. I kill it every night; fool myself that its sister will not grow tomorrow. It incubates in my sock drawer, grows in a jar like sourdough starter, reborn again red and wailing and I cannot decide yet if I am ready to toss out a life like that, even if it is not mine to discard.

II

The man's arms were full of women, and his eyes, his head, everything women, everywhere. His wife said, I was surprised to find how often grown men think about fucking. He nodded. All the time. All the fucking time.

They went together to pick her out. It took a long time, more than the one night they had counted on. There was more research involved, hygiene and discretion and that hard-to-detect-psycho-vibe, all the nitty-gritty the man had never imagined. Details were the woman's job. The first one seemed too confident, and the next too shy and the man got drunk and screamed, Where the fuck is Goldilocks?

The wife thought, Jewish. Anyone with Gold in the last name, and lox. There was one, it was the third night, and her hair was curly, she had braces on her bottom teeth, she was the right age, the ripe age of 28. She was not from New York City.

His wife waited in the bedroom. She was old-fashioned; she wore a negligee. He scooped up the Jewess—she was heavier than his wife, but so much smaller—and carried her into their bedroom.

At that moment, when he saw the fear and displeasure, earnestness and hope all struggling to erupt on his wife's plain and handsome face, he loved her so much he almost dropped the girl!

Please, Come to Tea

Cynthia Price Reedy

I filled the vase with a dozen red roses. Their fragrance didn't quite block the smell of marzipan icing, or was it the cyanide I'd laced it with? The petit fours were beautiful: icing smooth and creamy, colored a gentle lavender. I set the places carefully, arranging cakes and tea things, warming my hands on the side of the pot. Both chairs faced fine china plates, already holding the individual cakes. All that remained to complete the scene was the arrival—departure—of my mother-in-law.

The doorbell rang.

"Come in, Mrs. Middleton," I called, "everything's ready."

In Repetition is the Desire to Make Something True

Vanessa Kulzer

She knew her date would mistake her breathing for the rasp of passion, and she was glad. She opened her nostrils wide, pulling at the car's stale air. The man was oddly fervent. She let her lips be crushed back and forth. While not pleasurable for the traditional reasons, it offered some consolation. A bit. Slightly more than a grain's worth.

She imagined herself in another body, surviving on grains. An Indian ascetic, living high on a pillar, relying on the devoted: bony, and going without showers. Her eyes half-closed. What a glaze of enlightenment would brighten her leathery face! Then her mind merged her two selves and suddenly her date had his face buried in her ascetic's dirty beard. Off the pillar and into a Honda Accord. Her mouth stiffened as she corralled it into a pucker instead of a smile.

To distract him, she arched her back in the vinyl seat. The man's eyes flickered and he redoubled his efforts. His concentration was flattering. She watched him at his work. She slid up the cliff of his nose and into the valley of his tear duct. His black eyebrows were furry oars stroking in the pond of his forehead. She wanted to apply herself, too. When the rhythm allowed, she readied herself with a big breath through her nose.

The interior smelled awfully like McDonald's. "An olfactory affront," she couldn't help thinking in the voice of her father. That phrase, always the first thing out of his mouth when he came home after work. His shoulders working at the kitchen garbage bag, tying it's white tails reproachfully, holding the bundle away as he took it outside. Her father had an unusually sensitive sense of smell.

A bead of sweat fell to her waistband, was absorbed. Another false sign of passion. Perhaps she wasn't sweating, but crying from her pores. If he tried to get under her shirt and found the wetness there, would he be repulsed? She wanted to open the window more than anything in the world.

Movement beyond the windshield caught her eye. Across the parking lot, at the edge. Where the blacktop met a row of streetlights, just at the beginning of a wooded area. There was a running dog. His delicate ballerina feet machined by thick haunches. The muscles working under his shiny coat. A greyhound. Bounding across the painted white lines, in and out of pools of light and darkness. His slender legs opened and closed like scissors.

The man separated from her. "What?" He followed her look to the trees beyond. "Is somebody out there?" "I don't know." She continued to stare at the spot where the dog had disappeared. In the center of each ring of light, the lamppost was like a single birthday candle in a row of flat, yellow cakes.

"Maybe we should go," he said, starting the engine. The car, it seemed, would move her bones, weighted like piles of wood, in the molded seat. She saw her eyes in the side mirror, the brown irises tight in their shiny whites. The tires rolled forward, crushing gravel in their familiar way.

She Swam the Channel

Carl C. Smith

To the person who finds my body — I apologize for the nightmares you may experience after my partially-clad and bloated corpse bumps up against your dock.

I'm apologizing? I'm sucking in more water than air, and I'm apologizing? For what? For violating the littering laws? For leaving my corporeal remains behind like garbage after a picnic?

Of course, if you're a necrophiliac with a yen for a dead virgin, knock yourself out.

Very funny. Forget the fact I've been trying to get laid for months. Tonight was supposed to be the night, but my date turned out to be a loser boozer.

If it's any consolation to you, this was not a death by misadventure—just a simple case of chronic, and now terminal, misjudgment. The party was boring; my date was a joke. The summer night was almost tropical, and the lake had a moon river. I couldn't resist the temptation; I went for a dip.

Lyrical lies. Bad lyrics at that. The truth is I wanted to go home, and I was scared shitless of the gangs of teenage boys who cruise the lake road looking for lone females. But a little molestation or a friendly rape seems pretty attractive right now compared to the alternative.

I can hear my mother when she hears the news of my demise. "But she swam the English Channel," she'll wail.

Yep, I did—the Channel, a few Great Lakes, and about a gazillion klicks in swimming pools. There are medals all over my room at home to prove it. "She swam the Channel then drowned in a lake the size of a postage stamp comparatively speaking, anyway" will be a fitting epitaph for my tombstone.

Fact is, I did all right until it clouded over and the wind came up. The waves are babies compared to those in the Channel, but they're big enough. I guess I've been swimming in circles all night.

So, why didn't I stop? Why didn't I drown-proof until morning when I could be rescued?

I'm going to make one last try for the street lights.

Working Girl

Julie Ann Jones

By the time Germaine, a middle-aged *lady of the night*, who worked the city's red light district, finally reached the steps of the courthouse the noon sun was upon her. Already she had walked thirty blocks, counting herself lucky to have fallen only once along the steep streets of Birmingham's high rises. The glint from tall windows and parked cars split her head. She felt queasy from the heat.

"Late, late, late," she repeated to herself, as she sucked in her gut and puffed out her chest. Drunk drivers, check kiters, and petty shoplifters milled around the bottom stairs smoking cigarettes. A couple of men leered and whistled.

"Wanna have some fun?" cat-called a toothless man, mustard spilled down the front of his shirt. A younger man, good looking but equally unkempt, jabbed him in the ribs. Knowing they recognized her as a whore, she jutted her chin to cover up her indifference.

There had not been enough time to change from her work clothes; she still wore the red stiletto heels that matched the small beaded purse dangling between her breasts. Inside, her future was wound tightly and held together by two rubber bands.

"I'm coming to get my daughter today," she told them. The men snickered. A fat woman wearing a puffy dress with roses sneered. Germaine instinctively clutched at the purse, protecting the twenty hundred dollar bills stowed there. Her life savings. Money to pay the lawyer; money to show the court she was ready.

She stopped in front of the group and took a cigarette from the old man. Tugging on it she said, "Today I'm getting my daughter back. They said if I stayed clean for a year I could have her. My own mother wouldn't even help me."

As she bantered on breathlessly, the old man ran a dirty finger down her slender neck. "What's a whore gonna do with a daughter?" he laughed. The young man whispered something under his breath. The church clock chimed. She cocked her head counting to twelve. "Good." she said. She wasn't late. There was plenty of time; her appointment was at one o'clock.

"She's five now. She's been in foster care for two years," she took another, longer drag on the cigarette, and wondered if her daughter would even recognize her. "But now I'm clean and they told me that if I stayed clean for a year I could get her back."

Germaine surveyed the boy suspiciously—he was maybe nineteen or twenty—a good ten years younger than her. Once she had been beautiful and one of the best paid of her lot. That was before the years of heroin and cocaine and whatever else she could find to dull a pain she was unable to articulate.

Looking at the boy—first up and then down—she thought about falling in love with him. For a moment she thought saw a look of disgust creep across his tanned face, then flicker away. The old man noticed this too, and perversely nudged the boy closer.

Soon the others milling about grew bored and grouped off together leaving Germaine and the two men alone.

"You are kind of old for me, but your body is still hot," said the boy.

Germaine shivered. It had been a long time since someone had looked at her with heat. Inexplicably her eyes filled with tears. Men, tricks, johns said all kinds of things; she placed no worth in their words except for the payoff at the end. Now she felt the years fall away and she was again innocent and free.

The boy whispered to the old man who began to laugh. Suddenly Germaine saw herself raw—exposed. She flung away to the other side of the stairs and sat on the hot concrete. She closed her knees tight and hugged her legs to her chest. The boy followed.

"I'm getting my daughter back today," she said.

"Don't talk," he said softly, picking up her hand and holding it in his own. Germaine was taken aback by this gentleness and once again she shivered at his glance.

He tapped his pocket then pulled her up to her feet. "You need to relax," he said, and coaxed her away. Floating along behind him, she was ready for something. Maybe love.

The boy pulled her into the alley. He kissed her full on the mouth—something she hadn't experienced in years. Closing her eyes, pushing her body into his, she hardly felt the sharp thump on her head.

The chiming of the church bells awakened her. Dong, one, dong, two, three--she counted slowly to six. At first, she didn't understand what had happened; then feeling around for her purse it dawned on her. Gone was the money. Gone was the time. She had missed her appointment with the judge and the social workers.

The sun was setting. She stumbled up the courthouse stairs and banged on the doors with both fists. A security guard waved her away.

She turned to walk the long walk home. Looking back over her shoulder, she glimpsed an old woman in the glass doors. For an instant she felt a rush of sympathy, wanting to comfort her. But there was no time for it; she had to get back to work.

Peggy Guggenheim Visits the Fall of Paris

Sean Aden Lovelace

I can't imagine why I didn't go to the aid of all these unfortunate people. But I just didn't; instead I drank champagne -- Peggy Guggenheim

Most of what is said she doesn't believe because most of what is said isn't for those with money, especially now. The money is flowing out of the country, seeping, scurrying away, on foot, horseback, late night trains and airplanes and ships—stored in the States, or in Canada, but she still has her money and can get things done and she doesn't believe what is said.

Take for example chocolate éclairs.

She opens her umbrella and strolls over to the women huddled against the bakery doorway. Do you have éclairs? No we do not have éclairs. We do not have chocolate, they say, excited to share such news, yet scolding, shaking their heads. But do you have éclairs? No, madam, we do not have éclairs. There is a war on. A blockade. The British have our chocolate. We have none. Yes, yes, I understand—a certain method of smiling, a sliding twist—but do you have éclairs? Her voice ruffles with the wind, the yellow rain-mottled awning. A gray car passes and the tires hissing and she feels a tumbling in her stomach and the women look to the ground, to the tributaries of the cobblestones. Four minutes later she closes her umbrella. The women lift their chins from the coarse collars of their patchwork blouses and step inside the shop. She follows, the air layered and yeasty, heavy and wet with rye loaves, a tint of sour jelly, and somewhere, burrowed away, along the edges, a hint of cocoa.

Le Monde, Classifieds, May 23, 1940. Cash payment for information about mother, Simone, age eight-four. Traveling with large black poodle. Last seen at fall of . . .

She was sleeping with a commoner, not so much of any true affection, but rather in the spirit of social curiosity, a playful experiment in class relations. His name was Henri and he was a hairdresser. His specialty was hair color. She chose auburn over caramel because it matched the running boards on the Talbot. She switched to blonde while thinking of a time Laurence passed out during a picnic in a wheat field. (He didn't vomit, though—he had this talent for never vomiting.) Brunette was for Beckett's horrible suits, motley, often soiled, his grey-green eyes blazing above a rumpled collar. Red was for her sister Pegeen's perfectly formed lips, and the feelings she had for them. Black was leaning into gutters after long nights of drinking, John holding her hair in his fist, pulling it from her face. She's not certain what made her whisper, orange. Sore and refreshed, she stepped from his shop and the streets were alive but not in the old way—scampering now, heads bowed, no longer giggling, laughing, falling on one another to get there—and hours were long and faces unfamiliar and her hair pulsing, bright, fiery and loud through the dimly lit streets of Paris.

Le Parisien, Classifieds, July 7, 1940.Missing: Son, Bayley Pasqualye, age nine. Lost swimming canal at Boulogne. Substantial Reward. Please contact . . .

Are you an escapist? No, I've embraced our humanity—that's why I'm here, to see all of us, up there. Are you tight? No. So am I. I said no.

They would talk this way and the theater was dark and low and maybe not wet but it felt wet and they would sink into the swallowing seats and watch the bodies flicker on the faint blue screen and she would open her jelly drops, little pebbled strawberries, and let them roll about her palms, squeeze them flat with her fingers, pop them into her mouth. It felt good to sense her fingers. To feel the candy's weight against her tongue. The sweetness of the jelly drops cut the harsh pine of the gin, she told herself. It was a pleasing taste, not sticky or sickening, and she looked around for a sympathetic opinion. She turned to Billy but he was over there, whispering into the darkness, a humped shadow, most likely one of the whores employed by the theater.

What? What do you want? Just to know you're here. What? Are you tight? Are you tight calling me tight?

Whispering, hissing, yes, serpentine, and she stared straight ahead, her body floating with the gin. She listened to the muffled sounds, a grunt, a squealing feedback and she felt nauseous, fought it down, her mouth sweating, and she took a long drink, chased it with candies, and felt high and very low and so inside the theater, so dark and confined, so outside the world—billowing clouds, flames, smoke—and she stared at the screen, pale white on glaring orb on shadowed arch on shaved head, and she thought how visibly hollow, how plotted, how mechanical—sometimes they didn't even seem like human beings.

Why are they called blue movies?

What? Why blue? What the hell, Peg?

I just wondered. I just wondered why they were called blue.

Le Figaro, Classifieds, June 09, 1940. Father seeks twins, boy, girl, age seven, lost in market square, Abbeville, go by names of . . .

Notes on Contributors

 # Notes on Contributors

Sean Aden Lovelace likes to teach students and read good books and write when he can and canoe serpentine rivers and drink quality beer and run long distances. He has published here and there, recently in "Crazyhorse" and "Puerto Del Sol." He is currently working on a book of 20th century personas.

Ariana-Sophia Kartsonis' work has appeared or is forthcoming in ACM, Bellingham Review, Colorado Review, Denver Quarterly, Florida Review and Third Coast. She currently edits wordsonwalls.net and is a contributing editor for Scene 360.

Brandy Foster hails from the tiny town of Quincy, Ohio. She is constantly reminding her husband that the author and the speaker of her story are different people.

Ann Heide (B.A, B. Ed, M.Ed.), is an experienced teacher, author, curriculum consultant, university professor and content provider for educational CDs and Web sites. Ann is the author of *Active Learning in the Digital Age Classroom* (2001), *The Teachers Complete & Easy Guide to the Internet* (1996, 1999) and *The Teachers' Internet Companion* (coming 2004).

Tanya Clary-Vandergaag works with adult learners in Fort St. John, British Columbia, where she lives with her three daughters. In the summertime she travels to various festivals, slinging henna from a 1982 motor home and sharing her self-published poetry chapbooks with others. She has previously published in literary magazines.

Despite being born on the Plains, **Jason Nelson** still creates little odd worlds in letters. This very well might be his last print publication as nearly all his creative vigor has moved to New Media creations.

Ellen Parker's fiction appears in many fine e-zines. She edits an online literary magazine called FRiGG.

Jenny Ruth Yasi is a writer, herbalist, substitute teacher, singer/songwriter and housecleaner living on an island off the coast of Maine with her husband and her two daughters. She operates a pick-your-own-flower and herb farm in the summer. Her short fiction has been published in *Harbor Voices, Words and Images 2000*, and on-line at *realitytimes* and *quoththeraven*.

Janis Mitchell is a 31-year-old Canadian. She recently graduated from the University of Cambridge. She lives in London, England.

Oz Spies lives in Denver, Colorado with her husband Sean, their dog, Angus, and their cat Muldoon. She received a MFA in Creative Writing from Colorado State University. Her fiction has been published in several literary journals.

Julie Ann Jones is a stay-at-home mom living in Amless, Alabama. She prefers the quiet life of the farm with her pigs and chickens to the hazards of big city living. Known to be a bit of a practical joker around Amless, she has gotten the best of many of her more clever friends. This is her first published story.

Laura White Schuett has been an instructor in the English Department at Glendale Community College since 1994. Her writing has received recognition from the Mississippi Review and the Frank Nelson Doubleday Awards. Sheis a recipient of the Academy of American Poets University Prize, the Kuehn Award, and the Arizona Commission on the Arts Creative Writing Fellowship. Her work has appeared in Owen Wister Review, Northwest Review, Black Warror Review, Beloit Fiction Journal, and elsewhere.

Vanessa Kulzer lives and writes in San Francisco, California, where she tempts fate by motorcycling and eating raw oysters. She courts disaster in the name of art, including a dogged pursuit of the elusive "MFA" lurking in the shadows of the San Francisco State University Campus.

Dorette Snover graduated from the Culinary Institute of America in 1983, and spent ten years in Colorado as a private chef to the Rich and Eccentric. Since 1990 Dorette's writing has appeared in Fine Cooking and on NPR: she has also appeared on Food TV and PBS. She runs her own cooking school, *C'est si Bon!*, located in Chapel Hill, North Carolina, leads tours to Provence, and is finishing her first novel.

Julie Hannah lives in Texas, enjoys kayaking and her two cats who play in her workroom. The Siamese unloads the printer while the tabby wants to answer the phone, but has such a drawl nobody can understand him. Julie writes short stories and has a mid-grade children's novel nearing completion.

Katie Haegele lives in Philadelphia, Pennsylvania, where she writes for a weekly newspaper. Her essays have appeared in Utne, the Pennsylvania Gazette, and elsewhere. She studied linguistics at the University of Pennsylvania, and she often writes about language. She is working on a book of narrative nonfiction.

Much of **Linda Mannheim**'s fiction focuses on the ways that war and its aftermath affect personal identity and people's day to day lives. Her stories have appeared in Nimrod International Journal, Alfred Hitchcock Mystery Magazine, and New York Stories. She is the recipient of a National Endowment for the Arts Fellowship in Prose Writing and a Florida Individual Artist Fellowship and is currently based in Miami, Florida.

Kathrine L. Wright's work has appeared in New Orleans Review, Weber Studies, La Petite Zine, Small Spiral Notebook, storySouth and elsewhere. She currently edits the online literary fresco Words on Walls

Nina Gaby: Lucked out with good, creative genes. Has been a successful clay artist and psychotherapist, always writing in the background. But could not type. With the aquisition of a tiny Mac Performa, everything exploded. Has since upgraded to Vermont, an iMac and a Gateway. Owns a thirteen room inn with husband, daughter and Black Lab. Somewhat more successful these days at not behaving too badly.

R. D. Larson was born in Humboldt County, California, of pioneer stock, attended local schools in Eureka and attended Humboldt State and Sacramento State Universities. She lives on an island in Puget Sound. She's a former semifinalist in the Pirate's Alley Contest and nominated for the Frankfurt Awards in 2001.

Stephanie Sesic Greer received her M.A. in English from Kent State University and is currently an instructor there. She lives and writes in Cuyahoga Falls, Ohio with the companionship of one husband and four cats.

Lisa Selin Davis is a writer in Brooklyn, New York.

Diane E. Dees is a psychotherapist and writer in Covington, Louisiana. Her short stories, essays and creative nonfiction have appeared in many publications; misbehaving women frequently appear in her fiction. Diane and her husband, Orvin, are the webmasters of a site called Princess Café, which she claims to be "the world's only virtual rock and roll restaurant."

Mark Foss is an Ottawa-based writer whose stories have appeared in various Canadian literary journals and magazines. He has written a radio drama that aired nationally, and is at work completing his first collection of short stories.

Dr. Cynthia Reedy is a forensic psychologist by trade: her day job supports her writing and watercolor painting habits. She and her Scottish terrier, Elliot, live in Estes Park, Colorado, at the gateway to Rocky Mountain National Park, an ideal spot for both painting and writing.

Greg Lilly is an author living in Sedona, Arizona. After 17 years as a technology analyst in Charlotte, NC and after being warned that technical writing shouldn't involve characters and plots, Greg left corporate life for the high desert. He has published several short stories, and his first novel, *Fingering the Family Jewels*, A Derek Mason Mystery, will be published with Renaissance Alliance Publishing in 2004. Greg is currently working on his next novel.

Car(o)l C. Smith lives on a lake in rural Nova Scotia where she is kept amused by the antics of her canine and human companions. She translates science articles into executive-speak in exchange for kibble and birdseed.

William Bianchi lives in Lafayette Colorado with his wife, Jacquelyn, and his son, Garrett, where he works as a printer. He is currently writing an action/suspense novel titled, *Last Days of Harassment*. Bianchi is a member of the Dabblers critique group at the writing website, My Writer Buddy. He would like to thank instructors Melanie Tem and Edward Bryant for their willingness to share their invaluable writing knowledge. This is his first published story.

S.K. Rogers, an attorney and songwriter, is also the author of *Jump Cut*: a novel about love, sex, and electric guitars. She lives in St. Paul, Minnesota, her dog Cody, a former police K-9 who was fired from the force, fired from a security job, fired from an acting gig, and is currently unemployed.

Sally Haxthow is an award-winning Canadian literary fiction writer. Ms. Haxthow was recently named the 1st place winner of Byline Magazine's Short-Short Story Contest, as well as the 1st place winner of Wanton Words Short Story Contest 2003. She has also won awards from the 2003 Whiskey Island Magazine Poetry/Fiction Contest, the 2003 Writer's Repertory Short Fiction Literary Award, Tickled by Thunder's 2003 Short Fiction Contest and was short-listed in the Writer's Union of Canada Short Prose Competition for Emerging Writers.

Calabrese lives in Antigonish, Nova Scotia where she works in the Library of St. Francis Xavier University. Her poems have appeared in such literary journals as The Antigonish Review, Pottersfield Portfolio, Dandelion, Carousel and subTerrain. Her poetry has won numerous awards from competitions in Matrix, Other Voices, Zygote, CV2 and White Water Journal. Most recently, Calabrese was the recipient of the 2003 Ray Burrell Poetry Award.

Liesl Jobson is a flautist in the South African Police Service band in Soweto. She scripts and directs musical theatre as part of a novel crime prevention initiative in Gauteng schools. Her writing has been published in Literary Potpourri, Sacred Bearings, New Contrast, The First Line and in many ezines.

Laura Halferty is an Adjunct Instructor of English at the State University of New York at Oswego and teaches communication courses for the University of Phoenix Online. She holds M.A. degrees in English and history from the State University of New York at Oswego. Her fiction has also been published in Feminista!: The Online Journal of Feminist Construction. She lives in Oswego, New York.

Tracy J. Deobald writes to explore relationships and the reasons why we do the things we do. A lover, mother, mystic, activist and dancer, TJ loves to behave badly, or at least to fantasize about it.

Katherine Ludwig is a writer and fascinated mother living in Peekskill, New York. Her work has appeared in High Times, Vegetarian Journal, an e-zine, America Feed Magazine, and other publications. Her poem, "Criminals In Uniform" was recorded by the Brazilian heavy metal band Sepultura and appears on their album Arise. She is a former rock journalist/columnist.

Julie Paul is a Canadian writer whose work has appeared in various literary journals. She lives in Victoria, British Columbia.

Marsha Kysor Sray lives in Round Rock, Texas. She spends most of her free time serving on the board of directors at Sam Bass Theatre where there is never enough time and barely enough money, but always a wealth of creativity, talent, love and support for a burgeoning actor and writer. Marsha would like to thank Vic Kysor for teaching her the value of reading and David Sray for the priceless gift of his name.

Robin Skyler talks too much on her weblog "Ambiguous" and lives in New York

Annie McGreevy is a recent graduate of American University in Washington DC. She is currently living in New Jersey with her parents, and plans to move to Spain.

Robert Wallace has published fiction and nonfiction in The Raleigh News & Observer, the Bryant Literary Review, Reflections, and In My Life: Encounters with the Beatles, among other literary journals and anthologies. He is a previous recipient of a North Carolina Arts Council Fellowship. He lives in Durham, North Carolina.

Printed in the United States
17389LVS00004B/31-48